"NO, ADAM, I WILL NOT LET YOU—
OH, LET ME GO!"

"Why? Why should I let you go? You belong to me. I should have claimed you long ago! My mistake was in waiting—you will not grow up until I make you," he said thickly, his Polish accent very strong now. "I think you will love me, you already feel some love for me—"

She was indignant, ashamed that she should love when he did not. Yes, he must know it, he knew the world, he knew women. Her secret was not a secret from him!

She sought for words strong enough to stop him. She would not yield to him, she would hate herself for the weakness. "I know why you married me!" she blazed, pulling herself up with as much strength as she could summon, wrenching her arms in an effort to free herself. "You married me—for the money—for the cause!"

Also by Janet Louise Roberts:

THE GOLDEN THISTLE
LA CASA DORADA
MY LADY MISCHIEF
THE DANCING DOLL
THE CARDROSS LUCK

The First Waltz

Janet Louise Roberts

A DELL BOOK

Published by
Dell Publishing Co., Inc.
1 Dag Hammarskjold Plaza
New York, New York 10017

Dell ® TM 681510, Dell Publishing Co., Inc.

ISBN: 0-440-13237-1

Printed in the United States of America

Two Previous Dell Editions

May 1987

10 9 8 7 6 5 4 3 2 1

WFH

Chapter 1

"Well, Rosalind, what do you think of Count Potocki? Nice fellow, isn't he?" Barnaby Malloy was regarding his daughter with ill-concealed anxiety.

Rosalind turned to gaze vaguely through the windows. It was a lovely sunny day, this first of October.

"Yes, Papa, he is quite nice." What a mild word, when she was waiting impatiently for Count Adam Potocki to take her riding, to live in an uncertain fluttery heaven for a short time, to talk, to watch for his rare smile.

"And he is a rare gentleman, with all polite manners, and intelligent besides. You always like a man who is intelligent, right?"

"He is very intelligent, and very polite." And sometimes so polite that she did not know if he truly liked her or was merely being his courteous self. She stifled a sigh. She would not look ahead, she vowed. She would enjoy the day with Adam, enjoy her ride—enjoy the brief moments of his companionship, and have them to remember when she returned to England.

"And you are glad you came to Vienna, aren't

you, dear?" her father persisted wistfully. He came over to her as she gazed out the window, and put his long arm coaxingly about her trim waist. "I'm not one to push you, dear, but you'll be getting to twenty-three before long, and there isn't one Englishman you cared to marry, though I presented you at court, and did all those seasons."

"I know, Papa." Impulsively she turned and pressed her lips to his cheek. "You have been wonderful to me, and I am sure I shall marry before long and—and please you."

"Just so you are the pleased one," he said gruffly, his face relaxing in relief. "You're my only daughter, and I won't have you marrying a creature you can't like and respect. But you haven't cared a fig for the others, and you do like this Count Potocki, I can tell."

She flushed suddenly. "Oh, Papa, do I show my feelings?" she asked in distress. "I do not mean to show—I mean—I do like him, but he is a count, from Poland, and in society—and older than I—and much more experienced—I do not know how he feels. Oh, Papa, I would not be—be forward!"

"Nonsense, you are never forward! You are as modest as they come, and a nice housekeeper, and a fine woman. Any man would be proud to have you. And the fortune I have settled on you isn't sugar to turn down!" he added shrewdly, with a proud laugh. "Sure, I made my money in trade, but I'm not ashamed of it. And you helped me, many a time, after dearest Rose died. It is only right you get to choose the man you want!"

She heard the voices in the hallway first, and turned in relief to the doorway of the study. "There they are—he has come, Papa. Now, not a word of this, please," she begged, her face hot and worried. It was not past reckoning that her honest, hearty, impulsive papa would say something to the Count if he thought it would improve Rosalind's chances! And she would be embarrassed to tears if he did!

As Count Adam Potocki was shown into the room, she moved forward, the black riding habit flowing about her long, slim legs. At least she looked rather well in riding garb, she thought, even if the clinging pastel muslin gowns ill became her. And the high-crowned hat was right, with its flowing veil about her dark-brown curls. If only her face were fair and rosy, like many English girls'! But no, she was dark brown and sallow from the sun, and for the first time in her life she wished for sunny curls and a pale, pretty face, like her mother's.

The Count came forward, bowed to her father, clicked his heels, then turned to Rosalind. He took her hand, lifted it to his lips, seriously kissed it, and straightened upright. It always took her breath that he should kiss her hand, and she scolded herself that the touch of his lips on her palm made her weak in the knees, showing only that she was a foolish chit.

She made herself smile at him. "It is a lovely day, sir. We shall have fine weather for our ride."

"Yes, Vienna has excelled itself in its hospitality," he said, in his usual serious tone, but with a slight smile. "She has even provided beautiful sunshine and cool breezes. Are you quite ready to ride?"

"Quite ready, sir." They moved out to the horses, which her groom was holding. Grover, sedate and middle-aged, burly, and tough, was her usual escort, even when a gentleman accompanied her on the early morning rides she loved. "Good morning, Grover. She looks in fine fettle this morning."

"Ready to go, Miss Rosalind." He held the stirrup for her as she mounted. Adam was close behind her on his tall gray stallion, and then they were off, clattering down the cobblestone street, out toward the parkland that surrounded the rented villa.

Her father had searched out the grandest house he could find in Vienna, which had been quite a difficult matter. With the Congress of Vienna beginning, the town was stretched to its utmost, families crowding in, men bidding desperately for a rented place. Barnaby Malloy had not spared the expense. He was determined his only daughter should marry a title, and in Vienna at this time were more titles than in the whole of Europe, he had declared with immense satisfaction.

Reluctantly, Rosalind had agreed to what seemed his mad scheme, and had come to Vienna with him in September of 1814. Already it was crowded, but he had managed to rent a grand villa on the edge of the city, had hired help in addition to his own from England, and was set up to plan lavish hospitality in his daughter's honor.

Almost from the first day, the handsome, serious Count Adam Potocki had come to visit them, had escorted Rosalind to several dinners and two balls. He had paid her marked attention the past few weeks. As she was not a beauty, it amazed her. She had seen beauties throw out lures to him, and he had ignored them, or been coldly polite.

Now she stole swift little glances at him. He seemed unusually serious today, even grave. After they had left the street, to ride on the grassy paths of the nearby park, climbing ever upward to the heights surrounding the city of Vienna, she finally spoke timidly.

"Sir? You are most serious. Have you—were you able to see the aide to Prince Metternich?"

He turned his head and gazed down at her. On her smaller mare, she seemed small to herself, for he was so tall, and his stallion was huge. It was an unusual feeling for her; she was quite tall herself, and used to feeling big and awkward.

"You are most kind to inquire, Miss Malloy. Yes, we were able to see him, but to no avail. He said the Polish question is under advisement, and he could not make an appointment with us to see Prince Metternich." Under the courteous words she sensed deep bitterness and frustration.

"Oh, that is too bad!" she said, impulsively. "I knew you felt sad today. I wish—oh, I wish . . ." She bit her lip.

"You wish you could help?" She glanced quickly at him, but he did not look amused. "You are extremely kind-hearted, Miss Malloy. I fear it will take a great deal to reach the Prince, or indeed any of the high dignitaries of the Congress. They seem determined to ignore the matter of my poor Poland, perhaps until eternity!" And now the bitterness did ring in his deep voice.

He turned their horses upward, to the hills and the rise which overlooked the city. It was one of their favorite places in Vienna.

"And it has been divided and divided until there is nothing left," she said softly, appalled that a country should have been so brutally torn apart and given over as spoils to the three victors, Prussia, Austria, and Russia.

"Nothing but the people, and their fierce determination to be a free and independent people once more. But that might be enough," he said, his proud head high. She noted again the deep red saber scar marking his left cheek. She knew also that he still limped from the bullet in his thigh, earned when he and a Polish band of cavalry had fought with Napoleon. He had fought for years, leaving his homeland to fight abroad, hoping against hope that Napoleon would help them regain their independence. Now Napoleon was in exile and disgraced. The Count must start again to win the fight for Poland.

They drew up at the top of the hill and paused to gaze down at the gay, beautiful city below them. Vienna, the city of dreams, never so full of hope and ambitions as now! The Congress of Vienna had determined to meet here to settle the fates of the countries in turmoil from Napoleon's wars and settlements. Courtiers, diplomats, adventurers, men and women of a hundred countries, had swarmed into the city to seek the settlement and future of their own homes.

Adam swung down from the saddle and moved around to help Rosalind down. The groom moved up to take their reins, then drew the horses discreetly away while they walked to the edge of the small cliff. Rosalind found a clear place in the grass and sank down. Adam hesitated, then moved to sit near her, studying her face with his grave dark eyes.

"But I did not come here today to discuss Poland with you, Miss Malloy. Has your father informed you that I visited him yesterday afternoon?"

She stared, eyes widening. "No—no, he did not."

"I called upon him to ask about a matter of grave importance to myself—and I hope to you." He paused, and a slight flush tinged his cheeks. His lean brown hand was stroking the thick, sleek green grass carefully, very near to her hand.

She could not speak for a moment; she seemed to be choking. Was this the meaning of her father's questioning this morning? What could it mean? It could not be—

"I do not know—to what you are—referring, sir," she managed to blurt out.

"It may seem quite a short time, Miss Malloy, that we have been acquainted." His English seemed to be stiffer and more precise, and his Polish accent deepened as he continued. "But I have formed an attachment to you—indeed, from our first meeting, at the Riding School, in which you exclaimed about the horses—"

She smiled involuntarily. It was so typical of her. Entranced by the performance of the beautiful white horses, she had cried out her pleasure, and the tall young Pole had come forward and begun to tell her about the horses. He had begged leave to introduce himself, and she had assented. From then it had been one meeting after another, in her home and in the homes of others.

"We have a great deal in common, I believe. You are much attached to your parent, and to your country and home. You enjoy the pleasures of riding and dancing, even as I. And I have come to believe that you are anxious to set up your own household, though understandably particular that the man you should engage yourself to should be of some high quality."

She could not believe it. She turned her face away, flushing deeply, staring with unseeing eyes at the splendid city beneath them as his deep voice went on and on.

"We are both of the Catholic faith, and I have observed with pleasure your devotion at the mass. My mother is anxious to meet you. I have spoken so highly of your ideals, your devotion to the faith, your honesty and courage, your attitude toward your parent, the way you manage his home so comfortably and efficiently. She cannot believe, as I found it difficult to believe, that there is in this careless age such a fine, and may I

say old-fashioned, respect for faith, home, and
country."

"You—you do me—too much—honor, sir," she
managed to stammer. Her hands were shaking;
she tried to fold them in her lap.

"Not at all. I spoke to your father yesterday,
asked his permission to pay my addresses to you.
He gave me to believe that I might feel encouraged, and that I had his permission to request
your hand in marriage."

"Oh," she whispered. Her head was still turned
away when she felt a warm hard hand close over
her hands. He pressed gently.

"Rosalind? May I call you that? I would ask
you to marry me. I do not wish to press you for
an answer, but I have hoped so much that you—
that I—that you might—" He stammered, he the
most sure and courtly of her admirers!

She turned back shyly to meet his eyes, and
found his dark-gray eyes anxious. Anxious? Over
her answer?

As bluntly honest as ever, she blurted out, "Oh,
yes, yes, I should like to—to marry you!"

His face relaxed in relief; he bent forward. But
he did not kiss her mouth. Instead, he picked up
her two bare hands in his, turning them over so
that his lips could touch gently on her wrists. He
kissed one, then the other, and she felt a wild
thrill go through her.

"Thank you, Rosalind," he said gravely, his face
shining. "You have made me the happiest of men.
I hope to make you contented. We have much to

discuss of our plans; you know my mission here. May I call upon you again this afternoon, to discuss further?"

"Oh, of course, Adam," she said, shyly. "I wish—I wish you would stay for luncheon—you and Papa—and we could talk."

"Thank you, I should like that. And then I would bring my mother to meet you. She is most anxious to make your acquaintance. She does not go out much, being rather in frail health."

"Shall I go to her?" she asked impulsively. "I would be happy to—"

"No, she should come to you," he said formally. "That is correct. I shall bring her today, if that pleases you."

She wondered if Adam Potocki would continue to be so formal and so very correct after their marriage! He would be difficult to live up to! Marriage. She could not believe it. He—the handsomest, finest, strongest, most courageous man she had ever met—wanted to marry her?

They talked a little longer. Rosalind could not believe she was calmly discussing engagement and wedding plans with the man she had come to love. Then they mounted their horses and returned to her rented house.

Adam came in with her, and quite stiffly presented himself to her father. Barnaby Malloy was quite overcome with emotion and excitement, and it was embarrassing to Rosalind, yet very touching, as he had tears in his eyes.

They had luncheon together; then Adam left to prepare his mother for her afternoon visit. Rosalind fled upstairs, to try on one dress after another, fretting because she was not beautiful.

"Oh, Norah, I hate these styles," she cried in despair to her middle-aged Irish maid. "I look like a rag, a bone! This soft blue muslin—I hate it! If only I were beautiful!"

"Tush, tush, the Lord made you and loves you," said her maid, scandalized. "You are as He made you, and Lord knows this Count must love you, too. Can't you be satisfied with that, miss?"

Rosalind saw her face flushing in the mirror. "Yes, that is—quite satisfactory," she managed to say.

Norah hooted at her affectionately. "I should think so. The dozens of young men you have turned down. And now you find the right one for ye! About time, too! When be ye going to tie the knot?"

"Oh, Norah, we have just become engaged!"

"He might be impatient for the marriage, mark my words," said the maid. "He is no young one, either. How old be he?"

"He is thirty-four—he told me so the other day," confessed Rosalind.

"There now, he has been turning it over in his mind all this time! I told ye he meant business when he kept inviting you to all the grand balls, and out riding, and a-card playing."

"I could not—believe it," Rosalind whispered happily.

She did not believe it later either, but it was true. Some afternoon visitors she had quite forgotten about made their appearance at four, and had to be chatted with. Inwardly she fretted about Adam, wondering if he had changed his mind, wondering if his mother had told him severely he should not marry an English woman whose father had been in trade. She imagined all sorts of difficulties. And when the butler finally announced Adam and his mother, she quite jumped from shock.

She and her father went to the hallway to greet them. Barnaby Malloy, with unusual tact, drew them into a small private drawing room. Rosalind was astounded on meeting the Countess Constantia Potocki. She had somehow pictured a tall, formidable creature who would study her through her glass and make cold inquiries. Instead she found a small, frail, white-haired woman, leaning heavily on the arm of her tall, straight-backed son. When she smiled at Rosalind and held out her arms, the girl went to her impulsively.

Cool lips touched her cheeks, first on one side and then on the other. Then cool fingers held her back and gentle gray eyes studied her face.

"Oh, you are just as Adam described," she said in English, seemingly happy about it. "You look like a Polish girl!"

Rosalind flushed. Adam smiled. "Mother, you will embarrass her. I asked you not to make personal remarks!"

The Countess only smiled, like a mischievous child. "And why not, when she is to be my daughter? Can one become more personal than that? You are happy, my dearest one?" she asked Rosalind anxiously. "You love my son here, bad as he is, hard as he is?" And she seemed to hang on Rosalind's answer.

"Bad? Hard? Ma'am, you are harsh on your lad," laughed Barnaby Malloy, unconscious that he was interrupting Rosalind's answer. "One would think he has had a wild life!"

"So he has, so he has. Since our homes were taken from us, we have roamed the world. He left me in Vienna and in Rome for years while he went to fight, and he came home with a bullet in his leg, and scars on his face. Bad boy," she said, and reached up lovingly to touch the scar on his cheek.

Adam gazed down at her gravely, but with a slight twinkle in his eyes. "I shall not let you talk long to Rosalind, Mother, or you might frighten her off," he said, in slight rebuke. "Rosalind, will you agree to an announcement soon of our engagement?" And he turned to the tall girl.

"I—I think so, Adam," she said, a little breathlessly. She wondered what she would have answered if her father had allowed her to say whether she loved Adam. She did love him, she did, but Adam had not said the word *love* to her. Was he so formal, so correct, so polite, that he would not speak such words to her?

"Well, we have company this afternoon," her father said jovially. "It won't go amiss to tell them all, will it? Then we shall have an engagement party. Yes, yes, we must have a ball for you, Rosalind! It isn't every day my daughter gets engaged to be married!"

"A ball! Oh, jolly!" said the Countess Potocki

joyously, sounding like a girl. "And I shall dance too!"

"If the doctor permits it, Mother," said Adam, smiling across his mother's head at Rosalind.

Countess Constantia took Rosalind's hand coaxingly. "You will help me persuade him, will you not, dearest? You must have much influence on Adam now! You will let me run loose a bit, and not be wrapped in so much cotton! I know you will!"

When they went in to the other guests, to announce the engagement informally, the older woman clung to Rosalind, obviously taken with her. She sat beside her, addressed her in low tones, dignified yet gracious, and almost childlike in her bluntness. She had longed to become acquainted with Rosalind from Adam's first account of her, she confided. She was so sweet that Rosalind found herself quite looking forward to having the lady as her mother-in-law.

When she looked across the room to where Adam stood beside the mantel, soldier-straight, his head erect, his face grave and thoughtful, and considered that one day she would be his wife—her breath caught, and she could not believe her own happiness.

Chapter 2

Adam called again the next morning. He and Barnaby Malloy were closeted in the study for quite two hours. Rosalind was puzzled, but decided they must be discussing politics as well as the engagement plans.

They finally came out to her. Both were flushed and serious. She glanced from one to the other, biting her lip. Would her father become angry at something, in his impulsive way, and offend Adam into crying off? Or had Adam changed his mind about marrying the daughter of a tradesman? She was not ashamed of her father—rather, she was proud of him. And she would not marry Adam if he showed scorn of Barnaby Malloy.

She felt quite stiff and anxious as she served tea to them. She prepared it carefully as her father liked it, rich with cream, then handed Adam's cup to him, with its cream and sugar.

Adam smiled down at her, his rare flashing smile, and came to sit beside her. She was glad no visitors had come that morning so they could talk together.

"We've been talking over some plans, Rosalind," her father said, from the depths of his favorite chair. He crossed his long legs, set his teacup down, and reached for a plate of tea cakes near him. "Now, what do you think to have the engagement ball this Friday evening? I have spoken to a man about renting a hall, but I think it might be nicer to have a small party here, use the ballroom, and invite about four dozen guests. Adam leans to the small party."

"This Friday!" Rosalind gasped. She had scarcely heard a word since he said that. "This—this week! Papa! It is so soon! Do you not think

. . ." She turned appealingly to Adam. "Isn't—isn't it—very quick?" she faltered. His gray eyes were thoughtful, cool, studying her.

He set down his teacup and put his cool hand on her nearest one. "Rosalind, you know my mission here takes up much time. We had considered whether it might be best to postpone the wedding until after the Congress was over and we could marry in England. But I am impatient, and your father thought we might plan the wedding for next week. Then, when the Congress convenes, I might have time to do my politicking, as he calls it." He was smiling slightly.

Rosalind felt stiff and frozen. "Next week," she muttered. "Oh, no, no—not so soon! Next week—I cannot be ready—oh, Papa . . ."

It was quite one thing to dream of her engagement to Adam, to think of his growing tenderness to her. She could imagine them going to balls together, of how he would grow to love her, how she would accustom herself to his ways and manners, come to know him and his mother—

But an engagement ball this week, and the wedding next week! She felt quite sick with the shock. She put her free hand to her throat. It was so terribly sudden. She could not imagine herself being married soon—not even for months. And to plan it for next week!

"Not—not next week—oh, Papa, oh, Adam—how could we—how c-could we ever plan—" She stammered over the words, turned appealingly from her father to Adam. She did not miss the swift hard look that went from one man to the other. Adam's hand tightened on hers, crushing it painfully for a moment, then released it. He picked up his teacup once more.

"You need not worry about the planning," he said calmly. "It will not be a huge wedding. I shall arrange with a Polish priest I know. I thought we might be wed in the chapel here, where you often have Sunday mass. As for your wedding gown—"

She laughed, a little hysterically. "Oh, Adam, that is not the point! I mean—I mean—it is so sudden—so very sudden—we have not known each other long—and you—I—I mean—you might . . ." She stammered to a halt. She did not know what she was saying.

"Now, Rosalind," said her father soothingly, nodding at her reprovingly. "Don't get in a tizzy! Sure, the idea is new, but don't you see Adam is in a bind? He wants to get the wedding over—I mean, to get settled—before the Congress convenes, because then he'll get all tied up in his meetings and such. And you want to help him, don't you? He needs a hostess to plan dinners and such, when he wants to have the grand people here to talk to. I told him I thought he should move in with us, him and his little mother, and combine households. You can manage it all, can't you, Rosalind?"

She brushed her hand over her face in a daze. She was conscious that Adam was gazing at her steadily, studying her reactions almost with a chill detachment. "I—I think that is—a good idea," she murmured. "I can—manage, yes, certainly."

"Mother is not at all well," said Adam carefully, precisely. "I do not wish to burden you with her care. She has her own maid and cook, who know how to care for her. But I had hoped, Rosalind, that you might be hostess for me during the Congress. If I might invite guests here, feel free to have conferences here—your father has generously offered his study for my use—"

"Take it, man, I have no need of it," said Barnaby quickly. "And we can plan the house rooms easily enough. There is a whole wing upstairs that the Countess might take for hers. Right, Rosalind, the east wing?"

"Of course—the east wing." She felt in a complete turmoil, and her face must have showed it. Adam moved restlessly.

"This is all very sudden for Rosalind," he said to Barnaby. "Perhaps it would be best, after all, to postpone the wedding until spring, in England, when she might have her friends about her. And I shall be much occupied with negotiations—"

"Nonsense," said Barnaby brusquely. "Rosalind will manage! You both know your own minds— why, you liked each other from the first minute, Rosalind said so! No need to wait, no need at all! And your mother should have Rosalind's care! She's as frail as a little bird."

"I do not wish to impose on Rosalind's good nature," said Adam, more stiffly than ever.

Then Rosalind did turn to him, and put her hand impulsively on his. "It will not be an imposition," she said gently. "I was—very surprised, that is all. I shall love having your mother here, she is a dear. And I want very much to help you with the cause, to help Poland. If I can help in any way at all, I promise to do so!"

Again, a quick hard look passed between the two men. Adam finally nodded, and Barnaby relaxed into his chair, a self-satisfied look on his face, the way he looked when he had concluded a favorable deal in trade. Rosalind was puzzled, but her mind was in too much of a turmoil to sort out impressions now. She did realize her father wished to press the wedding, but his motives were a mystery. She did not know whether Adam wished to press the wedding, except that he did seem anxious to conclude arrangements.

After tea, her father said, "Rosalind, why don't you show Adam the east wing? Then he can plan for his mother's arrival here and reassure her that she will be quite comfortable."

On his prodding, she took Adam upstairs and showed him the large, unused rooms. "They really are not used now, that is good," he said, finally. "I was afraid that your generous father might be overstating the case. But there are many rooms in this villa, and we shall not be making anyone move out."

"Oh no, Adam. Father wanted a huge place in which to entertain. But we do not use half the rooms upstairs, truly. Why, you should see my suite! I have shut off quite three rooms of it, or I should be lost in it!"

She smiled at him, but he did not smile. He said, thoughtfully, gently, "Rosalind, I should like to see your suite. May I? Perhaps we might manage together there. Do you think so?"

She gasped, as though he had dashed cold water in her face. He did not miss her reaction, and a stiff look came to his face.

"Of—of course—A-Adam," she said. "It is—this way." And she turned her scarlet face from him, to walk along the hallway back toward the west wing.

She opened the door to her drawing room rather timidly. The room was furnished in her favorite colors, scarlet and gold, quite different from the dresses she usually wore of blues and whites and pinks. She noticed his startled look as he gazed at the comfortable golden sofas, the scarlet and gold drapes, the crystal chandeliers, the golden rug.

"And the bedroom is here," she said in a subdued voice. She opened the door to her bedroom, feeling quite odd about it. Only two days ago, she had not dreamed of marriage. And now—now—next week!

The bedroom was in pale gold, with a dash of scarlet and green in the patterned rug. The bed was wide, and covered with a pale gold canopy. A wardrobe door was open, and he could see the many garments hung there, her dresses and night robes. But at least the room was neat, she thought gratefully.

He merely glanced inside, but she thought he missed few details. He came out again and said, "Very pretty. Now, you said there were some rooms shut off . . ."

She took him across the drawing room to the far door. She opened it silently. There was another drawing room, a small dressing room, and beyond a huge bedroom . Everything was covered with dust sheets, just the way the owners of the villa had left it.

He looked through the rooms more carefully, but said not a word to her for five minutes. Finally, her face quite hot, she said timidly, "Should you—Adam, should you like these rooms—n-next to mine? It would be quite easy to have them aired and ready by n-next w-week."

He turned to her, and looked down at her gravely. "Yes, I should like that," he said, after a slight hesitation. "Rosalind, I know this is difficult for you. Please understand, I shall not make demands on you that you cannot endure! This is quite sudden and I am sorry for it. I would not have you distressed."

"I am not distressed, Adam. It is just that—just that . . ." She could not continue, could not express her chaotic thoughts. Then they discussed briefly how he would like his rooms furnished; indeed, his wants were quite simple. She promised to have them ready, and they returned to the drawing room.

The engagement ball, though hastily planned, was quite lovely. The huge drawing room was turned into a buffet parlor where tables were spread with a catered supper; wines and punch were served to the guests throughout the evening. The unused ballroom was polished and shining, and Barnaby Malloy had managed to find an orchestra of some dozen pieces to play.

Rosalind had chosen a blue satin dress to wear for the occasion. The pale color did not become her, and she was self-conscious about that. She had been working hard all the week preparing Adam's rooms and those for the Countess Constantia as well. She felt quite weary, and her face seemed browner and more colorless than ever.

Her feelings were not relieved when the stunning French girl, Isabelle de Guise, came in with her brother. The girl had black curls and vivid black eyes, and was stunningly attired in a white lace dress with full bouffant skirts. It was she who looked like a bride, thought Rosalind, greeting them with a weary smile.

"But Rosalind, poor child, you look quite worn," exclaimed Isabelle tenderly, putting her arm about the girl. Rosalind stiffened; she did not feel as close to Isabelle as that. "What is this I hear—that the engagement is this week, and the wedding next week? Why such haste?"

Her brother, Jerome, was studying Rosalind with his cold black eyes. He always seemed so hard, she thought. "We should not question, Isabelle," he said with a disagreeable, significant laugh. "She evidently wishes to make sure of her groom. After all, he is quite handsome and a count, eh?"

Rosalind flinched, and wished she had the kind of face that would hide feelings rather than reveal them. "He is—he is anxious to be married soon," she said in a low tone, flushing. "We—we have much preparation to make before the Congress convenes."

"Of course. The Polish question. You did tell me Adam Potocki is passionately concerned about the partitions of Poland. But didn't he fight for Napoleon?"

Rosalind compressed her lips. Their sneering remarks were not only in bad taste, they were meant to hurt.

Isabelle leaned closer, her bright black eyes malicious and questioning. "The marriage settlement must be huge, my dear! Adam is one of the most sought-after bachelors in Vienna! So handsome, so charming—and so poor! I only wish my fortune could match yours! I would give you a run for your money!"

Rosalind felt chilled through, as though a draft from the open doors had blasted into the room with a wintry chill instead of the pleasant autumn air. She turned away from them to greet the next guests, and her hand was shaking. It was taken in a warm grasp, and a gentle, accented voice said, "My dearest Rosalind. May I give you my best, my happiest good wishes for your continued happiness?" And cool lips touched her cheek.

Rosalind drew back slightly from the embrace to gaze into the wisely cynical face of Clotilde

Denhof. The handsome widow was dressed in black, but such a smart, sophisticated black—black lace over satin, the bosom low and revealing, sparkling with diamonds. Her red hair was swathed high about her well-cut features, her green eyes shining like emeralds in the candlelit ballroom.

"Thank you, Madame Denhof," she said in a low tone. The woman flicked her arm lightly with her black lace fan.

"And do not show your feelings quite so clearly, chérie," she said with a smile. "Not to those—dolts! They are cruel deliberately. Come, tell me, are you going to invite me to the wedding next week? I have adored Adam for years!"

"Who has adored me?" Adam was returning to Rosalind's side after a long, absorbed conversation with an associate. He gave Clotilde Denhof one of his rare smiles. "You, Clotilde? If I had only known . . ." And he bent and kissed her wrist.

"Naughty boy. You know how I have languished for you." And she gave Rosalind a mischievous wink, to show she was teasing. "No, no, I am but teasing. I am so happy for you both. I could see it happening—this love between you—and it made me so happy, I am quite romantic and springlike today! Yes, yes, I like to see romance blossoming between two young people whom I like and respect!"

"Thank you, Madame Denhof," murmured Rosalind, her face flushed now with pleasure and gratitude. The insinuations of Isabelle de Guise and her brother—that Adam was marrying her for money—had stung badly. She knew he had little money, and she had much. But he did like her immensely, he had said—but what *had* he said?

"Tell the dear girl to call me Clotilde," the woman commanded Adam. "I am sure we are going to be great friends! I, too, married a Pole, and we were immensely happy together." And to Rosalind's surprise, bright tears gathered for a moment in the jewellike eyes.

Adam lifted her hand once more, and kissed the wrist. "And you made him the happiest man in the world, as he told me more than once," he said gently, gallantly.

"You must call on me, Rosalind," she commanded, before making way for others. "I shall tell you about Poland and its people. I shall tell you much, and you may ask me any questions you wish about Adam!" And she smiled and moved gracefully away.

Rosalind felt a warmth then; she had made a new friend. She had heard talk about the woman, had been rather wary of her. Though of French and Austrian descent, she had married a Pole, and after his death in battle she had been a mistress of Metternich—one of many, but of some influence, they said.

"Are you not going to present us, Adam?" A jolly voice interrupted Rosalind's thoughts. She turned back to see a young man, with his hand on Adam's arm, gazing at her kindly.

"Yes, of course! My dearest Rosalind, this is one of my best friends, whom you have met casually

but must now come to know. Frederick Dabrowski. My fiancée, Miss Malloy—only you have my
permission to call her Rosalind," he added seriously.

The Pole—young, stocky, shorter than Adam,
but as smart as he in uniform—bent low before
Rosalind, took her hand, kissed it and murmured
her name. Then he beamed at her. "And you have
my permission to call me Fritz," he said provoca-
tively.

Rosalind laughed a little shyly, and Fritz
paused to tease them on their short acquaintance
and coming marriage before moving on.

An older, gray-haired man approached, and
Adam greeted him even more affectionately,
clasping his hand and arm with both hands. He
was introduced as Hubert Warynski, and she
knew that he and Adam were closely allied in
their efforts for Poland. He too was kind to Rosalind, and seemed to think Adam was fortunate
in his choice. It did much to soothe her injured
feelings.

Then she was conscious that the conversation
was being drowned out by the sound of music.
The orchestra had struck up, and the gaiety of
the first melodies rang out across the room.

Adam turned to her, and held out his hand. He
was smiling, with an open, happy look that
caused birds to start singing in her heart.

"The first waltz! Rosalind, my dearest," he said,
and drew her out onto the polished floor. She was
trembling as he put his arm about her waist and

began to waltz with her. They were the only ones on the floor as they circled the room. She could see nothing but a dazzling blaze of lights from the chandeliers, the echo of lights in mirrors, the beauty of ball gowns, the sea of smiling faces—all in a blur.

She was dancing with Adam, the man she loved, and all the world was dazzlingly beautiful.

Chapter 3

The Countess Constantia was moved into the east wing two days before the wedding. The moving was hard on her, though Adam carried her up the stairs and into her own pretty rooms.

Rosalind had consulted her hastily on the colors, and had worked feverishly to make them lovely. The gray and blue with a touch of pink was a delight to the eye, and a perfect setting for the tiny frail Countess as Adam set her gently down on the couch in her own drawing room.

She rested all that day and the next, so that she might attend the wedding. Adam was with her frequently, obviously anxious over her health. He had taken rooms with Fritz until the wedding day.

Rosalind moved in a daze. The dressmaker had come every day, and grumbled a little over the haste in making the beautiful wedding gown Adam had chosen. He wanted her in a full white

gown of lace over silk, caught up with white
rosebuds. The low neck was partially covered
with the white lace veil, which streamed from
her curly head to her waist. The pure white was
unexpectedly flattering, thought Rosalind in relief. The cream muslins were decidedly not her
style, but this pure shimmering white became her.

She had managed to cut down the invitation
list to three dozen guests. She wanted only close
friends of hers and Adam's, and she prevailed
over Barnaby's protests. He was set on inviting
every high dignitary in Vienna, she thought, as
she crossed through the names of Metternich,
Talleyrand, Alexander I— Dear God, she
thought, in laughing despair. Only her father
would think to invite the Czar to his daughter's
wedding!

She confided in Clotilde Denhof. "My father
would invite the King of England to appear," she
said with a sigh. "He thinks no one could fail to
respond to invitations to my wedding! Was there
ever such a proud papa?" And she grimaced. "If I
were beautiful, it might be different!"

Clotilde looked very thoughtful, tapping her
black lace fan on her palm. "Well—perhaps," she
murmured. "Not for the wedding, dearest, but
later on. Yes, you shall surely have a dinner for
some of them! We shall see!"

Rosalind had no time to quiz her on the matter.
There was a crisis in the kitchen. The English
cook they had brought with them had finally
joined forces with his enemy, the Austrian cook
they had hired, against the Polish cook the

Countess had brought in with her entourage. It took all of Rosalind's diplomacy to settle the matter of seniority.

"Can you not see? We shall need all your expert knowledge for the dinners and events we are planning," she appealed to them. "There will be times when English guests will be here, many times when Austrian dishes should be served. And I wish to learn much about Polish dishes, to please my new husband with them! How can we manage without all three of you?"

She was quite exhausted with it, but satisfied as they grumbled and finally agreed to remain and see how the situation would work out.

Her wedding day dawned bright and sunny. Rosalind longed to go out riding on her mare rather than dress for the huge event, the frightening event which would change her name, her life, her very self. She had to stand still for quite half an hour for the final sewing of the wedding dress on her, so that the waist might be tiny enough, the sleeves fit just so at the wrists. She was now wearing her engagement ring, a fine diamond set in emeralds. The golden ring would join it before long, and she looked again and again at her slim brown hand in wonder.

Her father came up impatiently, and paced about her drawing room while she finished her preparations. When she was ready, she went to kneel on the worn bench at the prayer niche and murmur her last prayers to the Madonna. "Oh, let him love me," she found herself whispering, when she should have been dedicating her spirit to the

faith. "Let him love me, oh please—let it not be
an empty marriage—please, Madonna . . ."

She rose to her feet, comforted, and went out
to meet her father. His anxious face relaxed as he
gazed at her before kissing her tenderly.

"If your mother could see you today," he finally
blurted out, and Norah burst out weeping.

"Oh, hush, the both of you," said Rosalind finally, tears stinging her eyes. "Would you have
this a wake? You would think you were not attending my wedding—come now, cheer up!"

"Oh, I am so happy," sobbed Norah, wiping her
eyes on her lace-trimmed apron. "Do have a care
of that dress going through the door," she yelped,
as Rosalind swept through.

Rosalind moved down the stairs with her father, and saw a few of the last guests moving to
the chapel door. Lady Sophia Eardley and her
brother, Sir Percy, caught sight of her and waved
happily. Sophia mouthed the word "Beautiful!"
and nodded her lovely golden head in approval as
Rosalind walked toward them.

Through the chapel door, down the short aisle
to the altar, where Adam stood with Fritz. Adam
had turned to face her, his face so gravely serious,
yet shining, that she could scarcely look at him
through her thin white lace veil. She moved to
meet him, and stood next to him, trembling a little.

It was only their close friends, she thought
again and again, through the ceremony and the
high mass. She stood, knelt, stood again, went
through the ritual as directed by the priest. But

only their close friends and relatives were there. No mean thoughts of Isabelle de Guise or any others must be allowed to intrude. Adam was marrying her because he wanted to—he had said so, he had asked her. He wanted her for his wife! He could have married any of many girls, everyone said so. But he had chosen her.

Finally the ceremony was over. Her veil was back, and Adam bent and gently kissed the corner of her mouth. Then he took her hand and turned her. Her father came to kiss her, tears in his eyes. From him she went to where the Countess Constantia Potocki was sitting in a comfortable armchair, her little form crumpled in it wearily.

Rosalind bent to receive her blessing, and found it in the tender touch of a trembling hand, a fond kiss on her cheek. "My daughter now," the woman whispered with a shaky smile. Then Adam bent to fold her in his arms, and received a fierce hug and some words in rapid Polish.

The reception was a blur. There was laughter, toasts, much wine and champagne, food she could not eat, a huge cake to be cut, some typical Polish foods prepared by the Polish chef.

Sometime during the events, the Countess was carried back upstairs to rest. Rosalind wished she too could disappear, and either rest on her bed or go for a long gallop in the countryside on her mare. Not to stand for hours in the full white gown, and receive congratulations and teasing and best wishes and discussion of where they would live later on.

She knew little of their future; she had not looked ahead. It was too much already that they had married in such haste. She could not think where they were to live later, in England or in Poland, in the city or in the country, in one of Barnaby's homes or in one of their own making. She did not know, she could not answer.

But finally the afternoon, and the evening also, began to wane; the hour grew late. And at last she was able to go upstairs to her room, to have the now-heavy wedding gown removed, to slip into a new white night robe of silk and lace, and the matching white negligee.

Norah blew out all but the last few candles, smilingly wished her good night, and left, with a significant look at the bedcovers turned down on both sides.

Rosalind went over to her prayer niche, knelt down, tried to pray. But her thoughts were in chaos again. She was happy, yet afraid. She had wanted to become a wife—but it was all so very sudden. Why, Adam had scarcely kissed her. He had never held her in his arms!

Finally she went to the bed, removed her negligee, and slipped inside the covers. She lay down on the plump pillows and waited, her heart thumping.

She knew Adam had gone to his rooms when she had retired to hers. He would be coming soon. She wondered what he would look like in nightshirt and robe. He was always so neatly, immaculately dressed, usually in gray velvet or silk, or in uniform.

Her hands felt cold. She held them under the covers and tried to warm them. She grew tired of lying on her back, waiting, and turned over and curled up. Still he did not come. The huge house grew quiet. She could hear the night winds murmuring, the rustle of the trees outside her window.

Silence. Still he did not come. She finally sat up and looked at the clock. Midnight. Where was he? Did he expect her to come to him? No, Norah had prepared her bed. Her maid would know— would she not?

She lay down again, worried, colder. Bewildered. Why did he not come to her? Was he angry? Had something happened to upset him? She knew little of his moods and angers and what would please him. That was it, they were still strangers to each other. She had not had a chance to come to understand him.

She did not sleep much that night. She finally drifted off into a brief, unhappy slumber, marred by nightmares in which Adam was fighting a battle with someone with blond hair—a girl? And Rosalind was wringing her hands and crying out because she could not help him. He did not want her to help him, he was saying he would fight alone.

Toward morning she fell into a deeper sleep, and was startled awake when Norah came into her room. She blinked, dazed, as the maid opened her curtains.

"Oh—Norah—is it late?" she muttered sleepily.

"Aye, that it is," said the maid, sounding rather

grim and cross. She thumped the tea tray down on the bedside table at Rosalind's side. "Quite late. Almost noontime, it is." She put her red hands on her hips and stared down at the girl cuddled into the pillows.

"Well—I was tired," said Rosalind defensively. "Has everyone had breakfast?"

She sat up and reached for the teacup. She was thirsty and weary from the restless night and the days before it.

"They have. And your father and your husband in the study these hours, talking away. Fine way to spend a honeymoon! You should ha' gone to the mountains, like I said!"

Rosalind flushed unhappily, and bent her face to the cup like a guilty child. "He—he needs to consult here, Norah. I told you that."

The independent Irish maid muttered something and turned away to draw Rosalind's bath. She dressed her tenderly in a white muslin dress with blue ribbons, and the girl went downstairs rather timidly to see what the day might bring.

The first matter was the menu for the next two days. So mundane a matter, and she had handled it every day for years. She bent over them, changed an item or two, made a mental note to ask Adam what other Polish dishes he might care to have.

Then she went to the drawing room, wondering if she might see her husband, what he might say, if he might speak of the night before.

She was alone. No guests would trouble them

on the first days of their honeymoon, she thought, with an ironic twist of her mouth. She wandered to the well-stocked bookcase, took out a volume, and began to glance through it. She finally settled down to it, until her father and husband might choose to appear.

When they did come, they had evidently been talking politics, for Adam was flushed and animated, and her father spirited.

"If old Wellington was here," her father was saying, "he would carry it off a sight better! Now this Castlereagh fellow is too polite! Let them have all they want, he will! He won't stand up to them!"

"Do you really think so?" asked Adam with a frown.

They came into the room, caught sight of her, and stopped. "Well, Rosalind, slept out now?" asked her father jovially, eyeing her keenly.

She managed a bright smile. "And glad I am that I slept, if you two talked politics all the morning," she retorted with spirit. "I hope you do not mean to discuss it through luncheon? If so, I shall invite a guest to talk dresses and balls and horseback riding!"

They both smiled and seemed relieved. She led them in to luncheon, and was quiet when their talk finally turned again to politics. More diplomats had arrived in Vienna, and the talks were about to begin. Adam was nervous, she could see, from the little he ate. No wonder he was thin and high-strung.

He finally turned toward her at the end of luncheon, and looked directly at her. "I regret, Rosalind, that I must go out this afternoon. I had hoped to take you riding in the carriage and show you more sights. But someone has arrived . . ."

"Of course, Adam, I understand. I shall go up and see how your mother fares. I do hope she is comfortable?" Her quiet voice seemed to reassure him, and he relaxed and nodded.

"Yes, she is most comfortable. I feared the wedding would be too much for her, the emotional strain of it. But she slept like a babe, her maid informed me."

Adam was gone all the afternoon, and returned home only in time for dinner. He brought Fritz Dabrowski with him, and the young bachelor made many apologies to Rosalind for coming on the day after their wedding. Rosalind only smiled, graciously made him welcome, and wondered secretly if Adam had done this on purpose.

That night also, he did not come to her, nor the next one. Finally, disappointed, bewildered, hurt, she gave up expecting him. He must have his own ideas of marriage, she thought.

She made the household work keep her busy, and with brief visits to the Countess, and longer ones to her friends, she managed to keep her busy brain from worrying overmuch.

Some of their first callers were Lady Sophia Eardley and her nice brother, Sir Percy. Rosalind had met them in London, known them only briefly, but when they had rediscovered each

other in Vienna they had become quite close. Lady
Sophia was bubbling and sweet, and rather naive,
in fact. Their father was something in the diplo-
matic corps, attached vaguely to Castlereagh.
Yet the two young people seemed to know nothing
of what went on, and could chat only of balls,
gossip, and horses.

"It was so romantic, your wedding, Rosalind."
Sophia bubbled now. "Wasn't it, Percy? They met
and fell in love right away! I shouldn't wonder if
they met over a horse!"

"In fact, we did, at the Spanish Riding School,"
agreed Rosalind, with a little smile. It was one of
her happiest memories, that of the tall, handsome
Pole coming toward her, telling her in his precise,
faultless English about the horses, gazing down at
her with his cool gray eyes that seemed to see
and understand everything about her.

"I knew it, I knew it! You both adore horses,
and Adam is quite the smartest man in the Polish
cavalry! I saw him on parade and I was quite
overcome, wasn't I, Percy?"

Percy nodded amiably. But he seemed more
serious than his sister, studying Rosalind earnestly. "It wasn't one of them marriages, was it, Rosalind?" he finally blurted out. "I mean, people
are saying—your money, you know. And he is
poor as they come, for all his being a Polish
count!"

"Percy, don't be rude!" his sister rebuked, but
her blue eyes were curious also.

"We are—very fond of each other," said Ro-

salind, finally, "and I think that is all that truly
matters. Papa is very happy about the match. He
quite respects Adam, and Adam—Adam likes
Papa immensely, for all their quarreling about
politics! And Adam's mother is very dear to me
already."

"There, I told you, Percy!" said Sophia, nodding her blond curls.

"Well," he said slowly. "I told them it wasn't
like that. I am not one to gossip, mind, but I told
them I thought 'twas a love match, besides the
money. Of course, I have heard that Adam Potocki is repaying some pretty large debts he con-
tracted here in Vienna. Not gambling, you understand," he added hastily, at Rosalind's wide eyes.
"Debts for a ball he had, foods, the house he rented, and all that. Just gossip, I expect," he added
unhappily, as his sister kicked him smartly with
her slippered foot.

Sophia hastily changed the subject, but Rosalind was trembling. She could not lift her
teacup for a time, for fear her hands would betray
her. Adam repaying debts? Why now? Had Barnaby Malloy paid him money to marry his daughter? Was that it? Could it be?

The love match she had imagined, hoped for—
had it come to naught? Had she allowed her
imagination to lead her astray at last? She had
been so on guard against fortune hunters. And so
had her father.

But Barnaby Malloy was so shrewd—he would
not allow his daughter to be taken in by a mere
fortune hunter, would he?

Still—the title. Count. A Polish count. Barnaby Malloy had wanted his daughter to marry a title. And Rosalind had not cared for the British titles he had produced, not the pallid, bland young men and older men who had a title but little character to recommend them.

This was the first young man Rosalind had cared to marry. And the marriage—in such haste—before she could change her mind or discover unwelcome truths—

Was this why Adam Potocki had not come to her? Had her papa really engineered the marriage? Was Adam so disgusted by his bought bride that he could not endure to touch her?

Chapter 4

Rosalind lay awake a long time that night, puzzled, turning over events in her mind. Yes, her father and Adam had seemed like conspirators, and her father had talked to Adam about the marriage before he proposed to her.

Had this been, after all, a marriage of a poor man to an heiress? She winced, and turned to bury her face in the plump pillow. The very thing she had dreaded! To be married for her money! To have no affection, no love, but only cold distaste, a growing impatience with her. Might he even leave her in time? He was a proud man; the marriage might be galling him already.

But he was devoted to his mother; he wanted

her comfortable. They had lived in rented houses abroad ever since the loss of their estates in Poland many years before. Would Adam marry a girl to have a home for his mother, to have money for the entertaining he must do to promote his country's cause, perhaps for bribes to obtain access to the great men he needed to see?

Rosalind awakened early after a restless night. The sun streamed in; the very air seemed inviting for a gallop. Perhaps it would clear up her nagging headache. She bathed without calling Norah, and dressed rapidly in her black riding habit. She would go for a ride alone; a lively gallop would help.

She stole out into the hallway, pausing abruptly, guiltily. Adam was just leaving his room, his face somber. He turned toward her in surprise.

"Rosalind? You are awake early." Then he gave her his rare pleased smile. "You are going riding? Oh, will you wait ten minutes for me? I have been longing to ride!"

She would have waited ten hours! "Oh, yes, Adam, do come. The air is so fresh and fine this morning!"

"Marvelous! I shall change and join you at once!" He went back into his room, and she went downstairs to the breakfast room. No one was there, but a footman soon brought her a cup of hot tea, which she swallowed standing, waiting for Adam.

No matter why he had married her, Rosalind loved him. She wanted to make life pleasant and easy for him and longed to have him feel comfortable with her—so that he might stay.

She went out into the lower hall as she heard Adam's boots clattering on the stairs. She saw he was racing down the steps, taking them two at a time, boyishly. She smiled up at him, and he came to her and caught her hand.

"I say—this is jolly!" he burst out, and laughed aloud, his face flushed and eager. It was the first time she had heard him laugh, and she started at the sound. It was so deep and happy and ringing. "I have been wishing we had time to be alone together, the way we were before. I thought when people got married they had more time to be alone, not less!"

She flushed. "I—I thought so also," she confessed shyly, her fingers clinging nervously to his. "I told the footman to have our horses brought around."

They went out into the sunshine, and Grover was just bringing her mare and Adam's stallion to the steps. His hard face relaxed as he saw them holding hands, laughing in the sunshine, chattering eagerly.

"Oh, Grover, isn't it a glorious day?" she said impulsively.

"Indeed, ma'am," he said, and held the stirrup for her. Adam put his hands on her waist, and she felt him lifting her up. Then he was in the saddle also, on his tall stallion, and they clattered along the cobblestones toward their favorite paths.

They let the horses out, and Grover pounded after them, until they were satisfied finally to slow down and talk as they rode. The air was brisk and brought color to Rosalind's cheeks, and drove her dull headache away as though it had never been. Or was it Adam's companionship, his hand on hers as he slowed the horses, his laughing glance down into her eyes?

"Tell me, Rosalind," he said, finally. "In England do you have such places to ride? We have spoken little of England, and your life there."

"Oh . . . yes, I know." They had spoken little about anything at all personal, she thought. "Papa had a town house for years, while he was in trade. We still have that house, in London. But two years ago, when he sold out, he also bought a place in Kent. The house is about two hundred years old, of stone and brick, with a small turret."

"Is this the one which you have been redecorating? Your father told me something of it."

"Yes, yes, I am. It is not yet completed. And it has a fine forest about, where I often go riding with Grover. It contains some wild game, though Papa does not care for hunting. Do you, Adam?" She ended with a little quick glance up at him.

"Hunting? I have not hunted game for many years. Yes, I used to enjoy the hunt." His face had shadowed.

"And there is a third house Papa bought in Bath," she said, rather apologetically. "I tried to persuade him not to buy that also, but he would, when he saw how I enjoyed the sea, and the life there. Papa likes London best, but I enjoy the places in Kent and in Bath the best."

"And you do like the country, Rosalind. So do I, very much. You know, I find that more and more we have much in common, do we not?" And his gray eyes looked down at her very seriously.

Her heart lifted in vast relief. "Oh, yes, I think so, Adam. I hope so." The Eardleys were only gossiping, she thought. Such talk was inevitable when a wealthy girl married a poor man. She must not regard it.

"I have been wishing to speak to you about something else," he finally added, as they rode uphill toward the view overlooking Vienna. He drew his horse to a halt, and so did she, her heart thumping. Would he now explain his behavior to her, why he did not make her his wife? Grover came up, and took their horses as they dismounted. They walked on ahead to a grassy place, and she sat down. She had the odd feeling of repeating history. This was practically the place where Adam had proposed to her, such a short time ago. But so much had happened since then.

She waited for him to begin. He finally settled down on the grass near her, and put his arms about his legs, staring down at the view. She had the impression that he did not see it. She kept stealing little glances at his stern face, the dark-fringed gray eyes, the red scar on his cheek.

"I am a very demanding man, Rosalind," he began quietly. "I am afraid I shall make many demands on you these next months. But as you are a kind and understanding woman, with much intelligence, I think you will respond."

She held her breath. "Yes, Adam?" she asked weakly. He did not turn to look at her.

"I want to explain a little more about my mission here. You know that Alexander, the Czar of Russia, has his own plans for Poland. He wishes to unite us again, yes, but then to have us under his own control."

Politics again, she thought unhappily. But he had made an appeal for her understanding, and she endeavored to follow his explanation as he outlined quickly and concisely the position of the various top diplomats regarding Poland. "I believe our hope is in Metternich. The Prince is a shrewd and hard man, yes, but he comprehends the situation, and is not unfriendly to us. We are just a pawn in many hands, but if we play our cards carefully, we may win our independence once more."

She murmured an appropriate answer, more absorbed now in his speech.

"I came to Vienna, not for myself alone, but as the envoy of a number of interested persons, all exiles, who have fought abroad both for and against Napoleon. All our old differences are forgotten. We must unite and fight together, or they shall tear us further to bits and nothing will remain. It is intensely important, Rosalind. Nothing must stand in my way," he said, his voice hard and serious. She watched his lean brown hand close over a tuft of grass and rip it up, then scatter it to the wind. "That is poor Poland, torn, scattered. Can we ever rebuild? Ah, but we Poles are idealists, we hope eternally."

There was a ring of pride in his hard tone.

"I wish—I could help," she said timidly.

"But you can, Rosalind. I wish to invite various persons of importance to your house—to our house," he said, as though he had stumbled. Did he not consider it his home? No, perhaps not. "You are a most gracious and comfortable hostess. In your presence, they will relax and be at ease. Then we can present the cause to them, and they may listen. That is how business is being done in Vienna these days. Not with sword and pistol, but with words, with influence, with bribes, with subtle diplomacy, making use of friendship, old families, anything one can turn at hand."

Something bitter rang in his tone now. "I think—I understand, Adam," she said, quietly. "I shall do everything in my power to help you. You must feel free to invite anyone you please to—our home. I shall welcome them with food and—and Hungarian wines," she added lightly, with an appealing smile. "I think you respect them the most, do you not?"

His mouth twitched in a beginning smile. "Ah, you learn very quickly, Rosalind! Yes, we like the Hungarian wines the best. The Tokay . . ." He sighed. "Before the present war, when I was home, we used to entertain—Mother would have such parties—the house would be full for weeks!"

And the smile was gone, the wistful look returned, and he gazed down into the valley of Vienna as though lost.

She was silent, letting him think and remember, wishing she could reach out and clasp his
hand and give him comfort. But he did not want
that from her, not yet. Perhaps someday.

She would have to live for that day.

A church bell rang out sharply, clear on the
crisp October day. He started, and looked at his
watch. "Ah, it is late, I have an appointment," he
murmured, and stood up, then caught at his leg.

"Adam—what is it?" She cried out in alarm,
reaching out to him.

"Nothing—my leg. The bullet is still in it," he
grimaced, rubbed his leg briskly. Then he began
to walk on it. "Nothing, Rosalind. Nothing. Let us
go."

She was silent as they rode back. He seemed
sunk in thought, or perhaps his leg was paining
him. But he did not want her personal aid and
sympathy, only her help in the cause. The
cause—always the cause—

But if she could help him there, and he was
grateful . . . I don't want gratitude, she thought.
I want love! But it seemed miles from her, as distant as Adam when his face took on that remote
look.

Before they reached home, Adam said abruptly,
"There is the ball tonight, Rosalind. You will wear
something stunning, with the sapphires, perhaps?
I hope to meet some important men, and introduce them to you."

"Of course, Adam," she said quietly. If only she were beautiful, it might do some good! But the pale-blue ball gown she planned to wear, even with the sapphires, would wash her out, make her look the more sallow among the beautiful fresh complexions of the English girls, the dark beauty of the French and Italians, the sophisticated smartness of the Austrians.

But she did as he requested, dressed in the ball gown and the sapphires, smiled at the men he introduced to her, tried to make pleasant conversation. Fortunately, she danced well, and several men were quite nice to her as Adam stood in corners and earnestly talked politics.

Finally she spotted Clotilde Denhof, and smilingly asked her newest partner to leave her with the lovely widow. He did, with some regret. The red-haired beauty wore a stunning gown of emerald green, and waved an ostrich fan of green and white dyed plumes, her green eyes flirting over the fan. She smiled openly at Rosalind, and greeted her cordially.

"Ah, my dear little bride, how are you?" Her keen eyes seemed to miss little, and Rosalind forced a smile for her.

"Fine, thank you, Madame. I—I came to ask a favor of you." They moved away from two gentlemen who would have asked them for dances, and shook their heads at a footman who offered champagne.

"You wish to learn much about Adam? Of course, darling, I shall tell you all I know! I have known him since he was a babe!" And the widow laughed softly, her green eyes gentle.

"I—I do wish to hear about him," said Rosalind, in a low tone. "But the favor I wanted to ask concerns something else. Madame, will you—could you help me? Adam wants me to invite important persons to dinner, to aid in the cause of Poland. If you could advise me . . ."

The green eyes grew suddenly keen and eager. "But of course! Intrigue, I adore it! Yes, I want to help Poland also. Let me see! What shall I do? We must meet soon and plan a campaign, yes? What a jolly thing, I shall plan a campaign!"

Emboldened, Rosalind murmured, "I have heard—you do have some influence with Prince Metternich?" She inquired anxiously, hoping she was not going too far. "If—if we could have him come to dinner, to listen—Adam has been unable even to gain access to him for a meeting!"

A little flush tinged the widow's cheeks. "Ah, yes, Prince Metternich." A slight smile curled her red lips. "He is fond of many ladies, I will say it. But he still has a—a gentleness in his heart for me, I believe! We were rather close at one time. Ah, yes. Hmm. We shall try it, Rosalind. Let me see what I can do! Shall we meet and talk again soon? What do you say we meet at some café in Vienna—I adore the cafés—perhaps tomorrow afternoon?"

Rosalind drew a deep, shaky breath. She felt as though she had gambled a large sum, and unexpectedly won. "Oh, yes, I should like that immensely, Madame!"

The green-and-white fan tapped her cheek

sharply. "Call me Clotilde! For though I am much older than you, I feel we have the same interests. And we both adore Adam, hmm?" And the sharp green eyes studied Rosalind's flushed face.

"Oh, yes, yes, I do—Clotilde. And thank you!" The shadow of a man fell across them as they stood absorbed in their talk. Rosalind glanced up, startled, to meet the cold black eyes of Jerome de Guise. She shivered, as though in a wind.

"Lovely ladies," and he bowed gallantly, his French accent strong. He held out an imperious hand to Rosalind. "Have you been avoiding me, Countess?"

Countess! She was not accustomed to this address, but it sounded strangely pleasant, even from this man. "I was not aware of avoiding you, sir," she said pleasantly, smiling up at him. "It is you who are always surrounded by beautiful ladies. One cannot fight into the inner circle!"

Clotilde chuckled, and murmured, "Too true, Jerome! You are immensely popular. Is it your dancing, your charm, or your wit? I wonder!"

The dark eyes softened under the flattery. He bowed again, gallantly, to the other woman. "You would overwhelm me, dearest ladies. But I am determined to have my dance with the new, beautiful Countess! Come, my dear!" And he led her out onto the floor as a polonaise was struck up.

She had learned this popular dance especially to please Adam, and as Jerome de Guise led her through the intricate steps, she glanced about to see if Adam might be dancing. And she found him, turning quite correctly and gracefully in the dance—with Isabelle de Guise! The beautiful black curls of the French girl scarcely reached Adam's uniformed shoulder.

"Yes, he dances with my sister!" murmured Jerome's voice in her ear. "Isabelle has captured the Count!"

His words were meant to sting. She would not let him think they hurt her. She smiled up at him impishly. "Only for the dance, I believe, sir!" she said, clearly. "For he belongs to me, by ring and church," and she held up her wedding-ringed hand laughingly.

He stared down at her. "More wit and quick-mindedness than I had imagined, dear lady," he murmured smoothly. As the dance ended, he managed it cleverly that they should come to a stop next to Isabelle and Adam. He turned to them. "Isabelle, I told the new Countess that you had captured her Count, and she said it was only for a dance. Is that a challenge you can resist?"

Adam's eyes met Rosalind's, seemed to note her flushed cheeks, her hair mussed in the dancing. Then he looked down thoughtfully at the black-haired beauty, radiant in rose and silver. Was he comparing them, to her disadvantage?

"I never turn down a difficult challenge," said Isabelle with a brilliant smile. "But—is this one so difficult? One wonders!" And with a laugh, she swept away on her brother's arm.

Adam said, "Are you weary, Rosalind?"

"Oh, no, sir," she said, automatically. He

pressed his lips together, frowning slightly. Was he displeased with her for some reason?

"Then let us have this waltz together. I enjoy waltzing with you, Rosalind. You are so light and graceful."

"Oh—thank you, sir!"

"My name is Adam," he said, as though correcting a child.

She flushed deeply, looked guiltily about her. Sudden tears stung her eyes. Perhaps she was really weary; everything seemed to be twice its size and importance. He sounded cross with her. She had thought to tell him about her meeting with Clotilde, but perhaps he might think she was interfering. After all, he had said nothing about her arranging dinner engagements, only about being a gracious hostess to whomever he chose to invite!

He swung her into the waltz, and she tried to follow him correctly, so that he would be pleased with her. If only she were beautiful and naturally graceful like Isabelle—or Clotilde—or any one of a dozen other girls! Why, why had he chosen to marry her?

Chapter 5

Rosalind went out eagerly the next afternoon to meet Clotilde Denhof at the appointed time. She found the beautiful red-haired widow holding an

impromptu court in the café, laughing up at one
man, allowing another to kiss her hand, listening
to a third. She dismissed them all airily when Rosalind appeared, however.

"Go, go, all of you! I adore you all, but my dear
friend and I have much to discuss of womanly
matters!" They all did seem reluctant to leave,
and Rosalind could not blame them. She was so
charming, so alive, so vital.

Clotilde indicated her chair and waved to a
waiter, who rushed over for her order of tea and
cakes.

"Now—we will talk!" she said. And talk they
did, about a proposed dinner Rosalind would
give. Clotilde thought she might persuade Metternich to attend, or at least his aide. She asked
how Adam had managed to meet the aide, and
frowned at Rosalind's pessimistic report. "No, no,
that will not go well," she murmured. "But we shall
see, we shall conspire, we shall intrigue!" and she
laughed gaily, as though it were all a game to her.

"I do wish I could help Adam," said Rosalind
wistfully. "I feel so—so helpless! And he is so concerned and distraught about the matter."

"Um—yes," said Clotilde thoughtfully, studying Rosalind's face keenly. "And you, also, you
are not happy either, are you, dear? For a new
bride, you seem quite—somber."

Rosalind flushed uncomfortably. "Well—it is an
unusual situation," she tried to explain practically.
"You see, we did marry so hurriedly, so that his
mother would have a place to live, and good care,

and that Adam could give his time to seeing the diplomats, and—and . . ."

"Men are so stupid," said Clotilde sweetly and finally. "Oh, well. One must live with them, because one cannot live without them, eh? No matter. I have something else I wish to discuss with you. Clothes."

"Clothes?" asked Rosalind, rather relieved to have the subject changed. "What about clothes?"

"Yours, darling," said Clotilde. "I am going to be quite tactless and direct, you see." But she was not that. She went on gently. "My dear, I think you could be a beauty, but you are not being dressed properly. I have studied the matter. You think to imitate the grand ladies and society by wearing those ugly little muslin dresses, and those pale blues which wash you out, and all the fashionable colors, eh? And they are wrong, wrong, wrong for you."

Then Rosalind did gasp. "Wrong for me?" She stared down at herself, in the soft blue muslin, the deeper-blue cloak. "Oh, I do hate these colors, they aren't *me*. But everyone is wearing—I mean, the dressmaker said—"

"A poor one, I am sure, or she would never have advised you so! Your clothes are expensive and in excellent taste—for a lovely blonde with peaches-and-cream complexion and the eyes of a china doll! But you are a vivid and sunny creature, tanned and alive, a good horsewoman, dark as a Polish girl. Why do you not wear red and yellow and crimson? Those are your colors!"

Rosalind stared at her. "Red—gold—but I do love them, but nobody wears—"

"I would, if I didn't have red hair," and Clotilde chuckled softly. "As it is, I wear emerald green, brilliant blue, black and white, the most startling dramatic colors I can manage with my carroty curls! But you, darling, you can wear every dramatic color there is! I see you in a ball gown of tissue gold, one of light orange shading to deeper orange and to red. I see you in a riding habit of crimson velvet! What do you say?"

Rosalind could only gasp, weak and excited by the very thought. Clotilde seemed so very sure. The woman carried her off to a dressmaker as soon as they had finished tea, and began issuing orders to the woman. Rosalind was shown cloths she had not dreamed existed—a cloth of gold in shimmering taffeta, a deep ruby velvet, chiffons of various hues of orange and red, a deep emerald satin that set off her dark curls. Clotilde kept holding the fabrics to Rosalind's chin, and nodding or shaking her head decidedly, choosing, discarding, issuing orders.

Once she said, "Now, your papa or husband will not mind your buying many new clothes, will they? You have no problems about this?"

"Oh—no, no, I have my own money. I can buy what I wish, and Papa was always generous." The dressmaker was fitting a long swathe of palest gold to her, in a chiffon so light it floated with the least breeze in the fitting room.

"The waist tighter," directed Clotilde authoritatively. "The bodice tight and a little lower. Then the skirt in layers of chiffon, so that they stand out. She has lovely long legs, that is another asset."

"Oui, oui, Madame," murmured the dressmaker deferentially, through the pins in her mouth.

"Daring colors, sophisticated styles, they will bring you out, the beauty that is in you," said Clotilde. "And hats—yes, a hat with a dash and flair—something tilted to one side. Let me see the hats." And she began tossing them about until she found several that pleased her, a large hat with a tilted brim, a small hat with a huge plume of rich green, a red straw set back from the head.

Rosalind went back the next day and the next, and soon her room was filled with the new creations. She danced from one to the other in awe, scarcely daring to realize this was for her— all these colors and dashing styles that made her look and feel like a new, different woman! She wondered what Adam would think of her. Would he like it, or not? Would it attract him to her if she was as stunning as Clotilde declared that she was?

Norah studied the clothes dubiously. "They sure don't look the style, but that Madame Denhof, she is always the crack of fashion, ain't she?" she murmured. "And those colors, they make your eyes sparkle, and your hair seem even darker, me darlin'. Maybe she knows what she is doin'."

Rosalind could scarcely wait to wear the new ball gowns. They were so gorgeous, so daring, so stunning, the colors so glowing. Meantime, she wore one of her simple crimson muslin gowns down to dinner—only to find that Adam had dined out with a friend. She was so sharply disappointed she could have cried. Her father soothed her uneasily, and kept watching her through dinner.

The next morning Rosalind determined to try again. She donned the new red velvet riding habit, of such a rich ruby red, the black hat tilted and shining with a ruby plume. She listened at Adam's door, but heard not a sound. She tapped lightly, then started back as the valet opened the door. His impassive face showed no surprise.

"Yes, Countess?" he asked.

"The Count—Adam—" she stammered. "Is he —is he in—I mean—"

"The Count has gone down to take breakfast, Countess," he said, and bowed deeply before closing the door between their rooms.

Rosalind drew a deep breath and finally went down the stairs. Her booted feet sounded loud on the stairs. She went to the breakfast room, and found her father and Adam absorbed in some talk which ceased when she entered.

"Good morning," she said gaily. "Do—do you want to ride this morning, Adam?"

He had stood promptly when she entered. His face cleared of its slight frown, he gazed at her absently. "Why—good morning, Rosalind. No, I don't believe I can. I have an appointment before long. But it is an excellent day for a ride, I believe! Grover will accompany you, will he not?"

"Oh—yes—thank you, he will." And she withdrew hastily from the room, crushing down her deep disappointment. He had not even noticed her new habit!

Grover brought her horse around on her direction. She tapped her booted foot on the step, thinking. She no longer felt like riding.

"Will you ride, mum?" asked Grover as she continued to stand there.

She started, and gazed up at the sky. It was slightly cloudy, graying. "Oh—no, I think it might come on to rain," she said in a subdued voice. "I think I—shall not ride today, Grover. Thank you."

And she turned, and walked slowly around the outside of the huge villa, along the terrace toward the gardens. She was not hungry, she was not eager for a ride, she wanted nothing, nothing, but Adam! She wanted him to see her, to think of her—she wanted the impossible, she decided. And to think she had believed Clotilde, that her husband would notice her if she but wore the right clothing! How women deceived themselves!

She walked along the terrace toward the open French windows, thinking to go into the breakfast room that way. Or she might stroll for a few minutes in the garden; it was lovely now, with the late fall flowers blossoming in crimson and gold and russet.

She paused at the sound of voices raised in heated argument. She was just outside the study, she realized too late. She was about to retreat when she caught her name.

"Rosalind is very yóung," came Adam's voice, rather heavily, raised in some anger.

"My daughter is twenty-two years old and knows her own mind! She wouldn't be pushed into anything! She likes you, I tell you! I won't have her treated this way!" Barnaby Malloy sounded authoritative, helpless, infuriated.

"It is my—my fault for pushing the marriage ahead. If we had waited until the spring—"

"Then you wouldn't have had your money, my fine lord! No, you would not! And you needed it now, didn't you!"

Rosalind caught her breath; her hand went to her throat. She felt choked, stifled. Money? What did they mean?

"No, I need it now, and I shall need more than ever, Mr. Malloy," said Adam, his quiet, steady voice lower now. "I am sorry, but the expenses are greater than I had thought. I must give out bribes, much as I detest the practice. And there must be presents here and there, and bills to pay. The dinner at the club for men only—"

"I thought you was going to invite them here!"

"I intend to. But there are other occasions— and you did promise to help me with the cause! I warned you it would not be cheap!"

"I know, I know! But damned if I like it! My daughter being insulted to her face by that damned de Guise—yes, I heard the female. What is she to you, may I ask?"

There was a slight pause. Rosalind could not have moved if a windstorm had blown at her. She felt frozen to the spot.

"I knew the de Guise family in Paris, and later in Italy," came Adam's steady voice. "They are tricky. I do not know at this time where their interests lie."

"Well, watch out for them! That's all I got to say. The girl is pretty, but all the more trouble. And I would not trust *him* far! Now about the money—how much you going to need this week?"

Rosalind finally found her ability to move restored to her. She backed up, and fled around the corner of the house to the flower gardens on the other side. She stayed there until she was chilled through by the brisk autumn air, then made her way inside, crept past the study and breakfast room, and fled up to her own suite.

In her bedroom, she tore off the ruby riding habit and flung it to the floor. She found one of her old white muslin dresses and put it on. She stared at her face in the mirror, hating the drab, sallow look of it. But she refused to put on any rouge, as Clotilde had suggested. No, he had married her for other reasons! Adam would not be interested in how her face looked now!

It was for money, the damned money; Adam had married her for Barnaby Malloy's help with the Polish cause.

She sank down on the bed, her face in her hands. Oh, the final, acute humiliation! To know, to know for certain that this was why Adam had married her—for her money.

All the snide hints, the troubled words of Percy Eardley, the sneers of the de Guise brother and sister—all were true. Her father had evidently despaired of Rosalind's choosing any other man—and when he found her interest captured by the older Polish Count, the handsome cavalry officer, he had lost no time to settling the deal!

Her father prided himself on being quick in judgment, quick to settle a matter in business. So he had done it again. He had managed to sell his daughter for a title, bargain her off. But he liked and approved of Adam, or he would not have done it. Or would he?

But Adam? She cringed, her arms tightly about her knees. She felt chilled to the bone. Adam had married her for money. No love in it, probably not even much respect. Does one have respect for a bride who allows her papa to buy a husband for her?

This, then, was why he had not come to her at night, why she was a wife in name only. This was why he did not kiss her or embrace her. He could not force himself to go so far. He must despise her. He must guess that she knew, that she realized her father had bought him.

And now they were already arguing about the sum! She stifled a hysterical giggle in her throat, and was startled when it turned into a sob. She was not one to cry, but now she flung herself down on the bed and buried her face in the pillow. She felt so unclean, so ashamed.

The one thing in the world she had dreaded—to be a bought bride, to have a husband paid to marry her, to fall prey to a fortune hunter—

After all her fine dreams of marrying for love!

Chapter 6

Rosalind felt in a very daze of pain, rage, and humiliation. She had never wanted to be married for her money. She had thought to avoid it somehow, to find a man who would love her. Oh, God, she thought in cold despair, how could I have allowed it to happen? She had fallen in love, and betrayed her own ideals. She had allowed herself to dream, and had been trapped. The evidence had been right before her, but she had closed her eyes to it.

And he did not even feel any desire for her, much less love. When she rose from her bed about noon, she felt as though she had died, or that something had died inside her. She washed her face, dabbed powder on her reddened eyelids, brushed her hair, and coiled it back severely, then put on a gray gown and went down to luncheon.

She was silent through the meal. Adam and her father seemed absorbed in their thoughts, so she jotted down notes on a nearby pad as she thought of them. To see to the Countess Constantia and her meals—notes for a dinner menu—planning the dinner for Count Hessendorf—hopes for the dinner for Prince Metternich—

She had jotted down a couple of Polish dishes and a wine list when her father's voice startled her.

"What the devil are you doing, Rosalind?" She glanced up to see him staring at her.

"Just some notes, Papa," she said quietly.

"Hum. Can't entertain you at luncheon, you have to work the whole time," he grumbled, with a cross look at Adam. She could not look at her husband. She felt so bitterly angry, at him and at herself.

"I was thinking about the dinner tomorrow night, Papa. I am sorry, I have some other plans to make. Will you please excuse me?"

They stood, gazing at her as she left the room. She heard her father speak sharply to Adam, but did not hear Adam's reply. She went steadily up to the rooms of the Countess Constantia.

The little lady was sitting up at a table, eating daintily at a bit of chicken. She smiled delightedly when Rosalind came in, her keen eyes taking in her appearance, her face.

"Oh, I have been longing to talk to you, my dear! You are always so busy!"

Rosalind bent and kissed the soft rose-petal flesh of the cheek offered her. "I am sorry." She could not be angry with Adam's mother. "There are several dinners to plan, an entertainment. I do not mean to neglect you!"

"This dreary Congress!" said the Countess with a sigh. "How long do you think it will last, Rosalind?"

"Some say a month longer, some say it could go on for a year or more. They are farther away from each other than ever, I have heard the gossips say."

"And not settling down to the business, with all the balls and fêtes. If they would but talk to each other! Aren't men sometimes of a strange nature, Rosalind?"

"It would seem so," her daughter-in-law said colorlessly, turning away. She gazed from the window at the brilliant autumn scene of Vienna, the woods, the gardens.

"But we must have a good talk and become better acquainted," said the Countess, rising and coming over to her. Her head scarcely reached Rosalind's shoulder, but her arm went affectionately about the girl's waist. "You have married my son, and we have not spoken of this! When can we have a comfortable chat?"

Rosalind tried to smile. Her heart was beating painfully. The hurt was too new, too fresh. She could not conceal it from Adam's mother if they talked. "Oh—quite soon, I hope," she said brightly. "But today I but came to see that you were quite happy with the food, with your rooms—are you quite warm here? Has it been easy for you?"

The keen gray eyes were studying her with uncomfortable scrutiny. The gray head nodded. "Yes, my dear, all is very lovely for me. But then, I am happy when Adam is happy. Shall we have a talk together quite soon, then?"

"Yes, soon," said Rosalind, and left to see the chefs and plan another dinner. She busied herself until teatime, when visitors were coming, and then went up to her room to change.

She was tempted to wear one of her new

gowns, for they had been arriving from day to day. She could wear a stunning gold tissue silk, or a brilliant crimson velvet which set off her dark hair and made her sallow face look quite exciting and provocative. Or she could wear an orange which was stunning and unusual, the bodice low and daring.

Norah was reaching for one of the new gowns. Rosalind stopped her. "No—no, I think the blue muslin today, with blue ribbons," she said wearily. "It is—more the style."

Norah clucked to herself grumpily, but held her tongue. Rosalind dressed hurriedly, and went downstairs to greet the first guests arriving.

Adam came from the study with Fritz Dabrowski. He was relaxed today, his face open and smiling. Rosalind scarcely dared glance at him, lest her icy attitude thaw. She moved ahead of them into the drawing room, directly to the tea table.

Adam came directly over to her. "Fritz was asking to go riding with us tomorrow morning, Rosalind. Shall I allow him to intrude?"

She did not look up, pouring tea with a steady hand. "I fear I cannot take time to ride tomorrow, Adam," she said coldly. "I am busy planning the dinner tomorrow night. But do go with Fritz."

She sensed rather than saw his start of surprise at her tone. She handed him the teacup and he accepted it and moved away. Fritz came over and told her how he liked his tea. He remained to chat a moment, but she could not be open and friendly. He was Adam's friend, not hers.

After a pause in the conversation, he too went away. She poured for the other guests, greeted an elderly Austrian lady who had some influence, and saw to it that coffee was brought for her. Adam returned to her presently and asked for tea for one of the other ladies. She poured it without comment and handed him the cup.

"Rosalind," he said in a low tone, "is anything wrong? Are you ill?"

"No, nothing is wrong," she said, not looking up. "Would she like one of these cakes?"

He accepted the answer and the tea cake, and moved away again.

Rosalind chatted with the Austrian lady, although she could not have said later what the topic of discussion was. Toward the end of the afternoon, as she drooped wearily at her chair, Adam returned to her.

He put his hand on hers in restraint as she reached automatically for the handle of the silver teapot. "No. Nothing more. Rosalind, are you angry with me for not riding with you this morning?"

"Angry? No, I did not go. It was beginning to rain," she said quietly. "Perhaps another morning."

"It did not rain this morning," he said. There was an awkward pause. He seemed to be studying her face, and she bent her head lower.

"Will you have more tea, sir? I should get fresh. I will ask—"

He let her speak to the footman, who bowed and went out for more hot water. "Rosalind, there is something wrong. Mother said you seemed pale and weary. You are doing too much; it is all too much for you."

"It is because I have not worn rouge today, sir," she said, her voice unexpectedly hard. "I should remember to wear color, I am quite sallow without it. I am sorry to displease you!"

Fritz came over to them just then, preparing his departure. She turned to him in relief.

"Why do you not stay for dinner, Fritz, if you have no other pressing engagement? I am sure Adam will be delighted to chat longer with you. And you might visit the Countess Constantia in her rooms for a few moments. She longs to see you, she informed me only today."

Fritz hesitated, glanced at his host, who was staring down thoughtfully at Rosalind. "Adam? I would not impose further—I am here half the time." He was half laughing, half rueful.

"A guest in the home, God in the home," said Adam absently.

Rosalind had heard the Polish saying before; it gave her a little pang. She remembered another saying Adam had quoted before her: "A good weapon and a good wife, that's happiness enough."

Did he consider it happiness enough? No, he had required money, much money, for his purposes. Her heart hardened.

"Do stay, Fritz. You will brighten our dullness," she said, rather coldly. "We have nothing grand planned until tomorrow night. You shall stay and tell us the gossip in Vienna."

Both men were staring at her now, as though sensing something behind the brittle gaiety of her tone and words. But Fritz bowed, and murmured his delight in her invitation. "And I shall promise to tell all the gossip fit for a lady's ears," he added wryly. "I shall not say in whose bedroom the Czar of all the Russias has been lately, or what was done in the park—"

"Hush, Fritz," said Adam, and seemed really angry at his friend. He caught his arm and took him away. Fritz flung out his hands at something Adam said to him privately. Did Adam think her a complete innocent? Rosalind wondered about that. She had heard the gossip. She knew what was going on behind the scenes at the Congress of Vienna. Further, she had lived in London society long enough to know of the shameless behavior of some of the ladies and gentlemen.

The guests, excepting Fritz, had departed. Rosalind left to retire to her own rooms. She could not endure much more, she thought. She sat for a time in her drawing room, with pads and notes before her, but with her mind blank of all except her marriage and Adam. How dreadfully humiliating, how awful—and how desolate—that he should not love or desire her, or want her at all. To be married for her father's money!

She finally forced herself to change to a blue satin gown, have her hair done up in a fashionable but unbecoming braided style, and descended to dinner once more. She saw to the changes of courses, to the serving of the wines, to the physical comfort of her guests, but heard lit-

tle of the conversation. Her father was roaring at
the wit of Fritz, but she did not hear a word that
was said. Though her lips smiled, she felt cold
and chilled.

The gentlemen were left at the table with their
port, and she was alone in the drawing room. She
did not remain, but went up to her own rooms
again. They could entertain themselves that
evening, she decided.

She heard Adam going to his rooms much later,
but still she did not sleep. She lay awake while
the bells of Vienna were chiming quite past midnight.

In the morning she breakfasted in her rooms,
then conferred with the chefs, and when time began to weigh on her hands she ordered the carriage and went out. She had considered going to a
dressmaker, but decided she did not want to, so
she merely rode around for an hour before returning to the house.

Luncheon brought several guests, and there
was no time nor need for private talk with her father or husband. No one was coming for tea; all
was prepared for the dinner that evening. She
found she could disappear, and did so, going out
to a café in the heart of Vienna, and sitting alone
at a table.

She sat and sipped the hot black coffee for a
time, watching and listening idly. She could understand the conversation around her; her German was good, her French good, her Russian fair
now. The talk was of the Congress, but not of its
business, rather of its pleasures, its dancing.

She was noticed somewhat at her solitary table, but in her gray cloak and white muslin dress she was not accosted. She thought she was not attractive enough to invite rude notice. She recognized several ladies, but they were involved with their own groups and the gentlemen who hovered about them. She finally returned in the late afternoon to find her father pacing the hallway.

"Where have you been, Rosalind?" he demanded at once, as she walked in slowly. "We have been wondering the past hours! Did ye meet a friend, that Madame Denhof?"

Adam came from the study at the sound of voices. "You are finally home, Rosalind?" His Polish accent was stiffer than usual, his eyes also concerned. He came and took her hand. "Your hand—it is cold. Where have you been?"

She withdrew her hand abruptly. "I went out—to a café for a time." She tried to speak lightly. "I heard much amusing gossip. The cafés of Vienna are quite—amusing," she ended flatly, and turned toward the stairs.

Adam frowned. "I wish you had informed me you wished to go out. I would have accompanied you. I do not approve of your going out alone! There are many scoundrels about. Why did you not take your maid?"

"Because I did not wish to," she said, without turning her head toward him. She began to mount the stairs. She heard a little gasp from one of the footmen in the hallway, but she cared not.

Norah had set out one of the new dresses. She fingered it, tempted. The crimson did set off her

hair and eyes. But what did it matter? She put
the dress away and took out a pretty pink one.
Norah clucked at her.

"That pink does nothing for ye, miss, and well
you know it!" she said. "Now, why will ye not
take the advice of that lady and wear the clothes
she says? Eh? What's the matter with ye? Why
are ye turning so willful?"

Rosalind shrugged, and went to add color to
her cheeks. It did seem to help, though the pale
pink washed her right out again. She went down
to dinner, and sat silently while Adam entertained the important German princeling who had
deigned to come to dinner. He was so full of his
own importance that he was actually funny, this
stiff German with his pouter-pigeon chest and his
pompous speech. But Rosalind could not laugh.

There were ladies for dinner that evening, so it
was necessary for Rosalind to lead them to the
drawing room later, and entertain them while the
gentlemen talked politics over their cigars and
port. She found it an intense effort. Two of the
ladies were evidently old friends of Adam's, and
questioned her curiously and somewhat impertinently on how long they had been acquainted,
how sudden the marriage had been.

The conversation finally turned to the Congress, and she was relieved of the necessity of
speaking. Everyone had her opinions, each lady
had her own bit of gossip to relate with relish and
wit. The Czar Alexander had been seen coming
from the bedroom of the Princess So-and-So. She

would not name her, but it was someone they all knew, and Talleyrand had said sarcastically—

"But he himself is quite a rogue," said another lady. "All France knows that Talleyrand, even while he was a priest—"

And so the talk flowed. They had much to discuss, and Rosalind could sit back, with only the coffee to pour, and wish she could be alone again.

The evening seemed to drag interminably. The gentlemen rejoined them, accepted coffee, conversed, stood with various ladies or sat devotedly beside them. She noted that Adam kept glancing at her worriedly, but she kept her gaze downcast, and her attention on the coffee and brandy. He wanted a hostess and that was what he had.

It was quite late before she was able to retire. She heard Adam pacing the floor of his room before she went to her bedroom. Norah undressed her silently and left her.

Again she was unable to sleep until quite late. This was marriage, she thought bitterly, stuffing another soft pillow under her head. Alone, alone, alone, as ever. No one to understand and love her but her devoted, blundering father. And she had dared to dream of a marriage of love and shared emotions, the meeting of minds and souls.

She ate breakfast again in her own bedroom. She did not want to see anyone, and was reluctant to leave the room. She would become quite a recluse, she thought with a grimace. Perhaps she should never have thought of marriage at all, since she had proved so particular.

She had another thought. What if Adam's hopes died—what if he gave up, what if he wanted a divorce when he was unable to win out for his Polish cause? He would have no need of a rich heiress wife then. What then? She could return to England, retire to the house in Kent, live there in the country with the dogs and horses, and wander the hills alone on her mare. She had no further wish for society; she hated it.

How long? Perhaps another month or two, that was all. Then she might offer Adam a divorce, and a money settlement, so he could take care of his mother. That was all, that would be the end.

Norah came to her at mid-morning. "The Countess Constantia asks if you might come to see her today."

"Oh—is anything wrong?" Rosalind was anxious at once, and started up.

"No, no, don't ye fret! She is fine. She is just restless, and said you had promised her a little talk. Why don't ye go this morning and set her mind at ease? She is a sweet little thing—so tiny, a puff of wind might blow her away."

Rosalind went over to the other wing and knocked at the door of the living room. She was admitted at once by the elderly Polish maid, who beamed when she saw her and said something in Polish.

"She wishes you welcome," called the Countess. "And so do I, my dear. Come in, come in!" And she started to rise from her chair.

"No, don't get up, please. I'll come to you," said Rosalind, and came over to kiss her cheek. A gentle hand pressed her down to the hassock at the feet of the frail lady.

"Do sit here beside me, where I can see your face, dearest," said the Countess. "I have been longing for a good, long chat."

Rosalind stiffened, but no inquisition followed. The Countess wanted to talk, it seemed. She told her about the old days in Poland, how they had wandered from country to country while Adam fought for the Polish cause, and battled reluctantly in the wars of Napoleon.

"He is my only son," she concluded, with a little sigh. "I want to see him happy. I wanted only his joy. But what does he do? He worries about, scowls and frets. We have lost our home in Poland, yes, but we have our lives, each other, and now he has you. What more can he wish to have? God has been good to us, we have love and warmth and dear ones about us. Is that not enough? Do you not think so, dearest Rosalind?" And the gentle, troubled gray eyes studied hers.

"I should think so, for women," said Rosalind, in an attempt at humor. "But men seem always to want more, to fight for something, to battle and all—I don't know."

"I neither! I want to see Adam settled and happy with—with a son of his own. Yes, that is what I want. Then he will know what true joy is, in the carrying on of our line. I should like for him to regain our home in Poland—but if that is not God's will, so be it. What is more important is for Adam to have a home, and what is a home? It is a roof over one's head, the wife beside one, the son in one's arms. Eh? Is that not so?"

Rosalind leaned her head against the soft palm stroking her cheek, and held back her tears with an intense effort. "Yes, yes, I—I think s-so."

"Yes, I knew you did. I was so afraid at times that Adam would marry a silly chit of a girl, like those ones who followed him about. He is so handsome and so fine!" Her tone rang with her pride. "But he chose you, so gentle, so sweet, so much a lady. And I was so happy. Now Adam will be happy also. This is what I want for him, his joy, his peace, his family."

Rosalind was deeply moved in spite of herself. The gentle appeal implicit in the words could not fail to reach her. The Countess might know or guess that things were going badly for her beloved son. Or she might not know, shut off from the rest of the household by her own frail health. But her trusting words, her deep love for Adam made their own approach to Rosalind. Rosalind could not refuse to listen as the mother went on speaking longingly of her hopes for the future of her only son. He might become an important diplomat, he might become the lord of his own estates in Poland again, or he might live in exile in England and become important in London.

But wherever he was, the mother was confident he would be great. And, more important, she wished for him to be happy—with his wife.

Chapter 7

Rosalind fought herself. She did not want to be moved by the appeal of the Countess. She half suspected Adam had spoken to his mother and asked her to make such an appeal. But again— Adam was a proud man. He would do his own talking, his own persuading. And he seemed to consider it unnecessary to persuade Rosalind about anything. Indeed, they scarcely ever spoke to each other anymore, except in polite conversation before other people.

No, it was the Countess herself who had sensed something was wrong, Rosalind thought. Adam had married her to win her help in his cause. If that was all he wanted from her, well—she would try to give it to him.

By chance, Clotilde Denhof came to tea the following afternoon. Rosalind had scarcely spoken to Adam, her cold reserve lasting whenever she thought of his words to her father. Anything approaching a confidential conversation would be extremely difficult for her.

But Clotilde had no compulsion to be silent. She came, saw, spoke to Rosalind. "My dear girl, why are you wearing that dreadful gown?" she said bluntly. "I thought you had many more stunning dresses now. Why, why, why?"

Rosalind flushed defensively, and smoothed the

blue muslin. "It is—the style," she said lamely.

No one could say "La!" the way Clotilde could. It exploded in a little burst of impatience. "I am irritated with you, my dear! You could be more than beautiful, you could be stunning. Why do you not try?" Her keen green eyes studied Rosalind. "Someone has made you unhappy? You are fretting? Things are not going well?"

Rosalind decided to try a small part of deception. "As a matter of fact, they are not, Clotilde," she said, with a show of frankness. "Adam is quite worried. He has not yet gained entrée to the aide of Prince Metternich."

"La! Is that all! I must take a hand. An aide? No, no, we shall obtain the Prince himself. And you shall wear your most stunning gown. Has the crimson and orange arrived yet?"

Rosalind had to admit the silk and satin creation had arrived, and was in her wardrobe. "Good, good," said Clotilde, with immense satisfaction. "You shall wear it, and a fillet of scarlet in your curls. I shall arrive early to arrange all!"

"Arrange what?"

"La! Child, the dinner for Metternich, your hair, your gown! Let me see. I shall see him the day after tomorrow—no, that is too long. I am impatient. I shall send him a note for this evening! Yes, I shall let you know when he may come to dinner. A little group, perhaps twenty? Yes, I think so. Dinner, and some excellent Hungarian wine, a Polish dinner, I think, my dear! He will be prepared then to listen to Adam!"

Rosalind dared not hope, but her new friend

was as good to her word as she was frank. The following morning a note was delivered to Rosalind. Clotilde had obtained Metternich's permission to invite him to a dinner two nights hence!

She sat down abruptly on a chair in the drawing room, staring at the elegant script of her friend. Two nights? For such an occasion?

"And you shall wear the crimson gown!" added the note impishly.

Rosalind gathered up her courage and went to Adam's study. He had been closeted for two hours with Hubert Warynski and Fritz Dabrowski. She tapped on the door timidly, heard Adam's deep voice calling to come in.

She opened the door and entered. Adam's dark-gray eyes met hers from across the room. He stood up at once, as did the other two. She closed the door after her, advanced across the carpet. She wished, too late, that she had paused to change. She still wore the pale-blue muslin she had come to detest.

The gentlemen greeted her by kissing her hand. She was still not accustomed to that, but they were always very polite and with stiff manners which were a part of their heritage. Always they must be exactly proper, greeting their hostess, taking leave of her, thanking her for the dinner, and so on. It seemed the Polish way.

There was a question in Adam's eyes. She finally was able to turn to him, the note still clutched in her long slim brown hand. "Adam, I beg your forgiveness for interrupting your business conversation." She thought, They are affecting my speech! I am much more polite than I ever was!

"Of course, my dear. But you do not interrupt. We are glad of your presence. Will you not be seated?" He drew out one of the leather chairs for her, so she could be seated near the desk.

"I have received a message from Madame Denhof. She—she has arranged—that Prince Metternich is to dine with us on Thursday evening!" Her voice quavered over the words. She could still not quite believe it

Adam stared. She felt the others staring also. There was a pause. Adam finally said, "Thursday—evening? This week? He will— dine—"

"Yes." Rosalind glanced down at the note, reading the brief lines again. "Madame Denhof has arranged it, with my consent, of course. She will come, also the de Guises, and she suggested several others who are particular friends of the Prince."

"Coming to dine—here?" Hubert Warynski sounded stupefied. "But—but we were just discussing how to storm him! We cannot get in to see him! And he—he is coming here?"

"May I see the note, Rosalind?" Adam's lean brown hand reached out for it. She gave it to him. He scanned the lines quickly, passed his hand over his face. He began to smile. "But—it is quite so! This Thursday evening—dinner at seven—the Prince may have to leave early for a meeting— but this is magnificent! Rosalind, how did you manage this? We have been going round and round trying to think how to meet him!"

She felt a little dizzy at his delight and admiration. "It—it was Clotilde," she said weakly.

"She would not trouble herself if she were not fond of your wife, Adam," said Warynski, his gray hair ruffled by the many times his hand had passed through it. "This is amazing—beyond belief. Two ladies manage in a note what we have struggled to accomplish for months! Amazing!" His tone held affection and irony.

"But I must plan—oh, Adam. I thought perhaps Polish dishes—the chef will assist me—and the Hungarian wines. And brandy later. Do you wish to choose—" Rosalind eyed her husband with timid anxiety.

"No, no, I shall never dare interfere!" he said, his smile flashing. "You shall manage everything! You will do it much better than I! I leave it all in your immensely capable hands!" Unexpectedly, he came around the desk, picked up her hands, and kissed the wrists.

It was the first he had touched her for days. She flushed vividly, jumped up, and stammered that she must go and see about the dinner and the table ornaments. The men beamed after her, and she heard the excited talk commencing before she had closed the door to the study.

She and the chef planned the dinner at once, and he set out to shop for some of the items he needed. She returned to her drawing room, to dispatch by the footman notes of invitation to several friends on whom she could depend.

She wrote also to Clotilde, thanking her and begging for more help in arrangements. "For the dinner table must be at its finest. What does he like? What flowers, what colors? Oh, pray assist me, dearest friend! I shall wear whatever dress you tell me, even if it is a gray sack!"

Clotilde came around that very afternoon, with much practical assistance. She informed Rosalind that Prince Metternich had most elaborate tastes, that he was vain and loved flattery, that he adored talking above all else. "So keep the flower arrangements low, so he may speak to the entire table and tell everyone his views on all matters in the world!"

She was aware of Rosalind's wide eyes regarding her in astonishment, and burst out into laughter. "But you—you do admire him," said Rosalind.

"Of course I do! But admiration does not make me blind! My dear Clément has faults, as do all men. He is pompous. I am sure he will wear his jewel of the Golden Fleece. He will speak in all his many languages, to show off his gift for them. When he writes me a letter, it is a book! He knows his own judgment is always the best, he knows he has always had the utmost foresight in all matters. But with all this, he is a dear to me!"

"Indeed!" said Rosalind very feebly, rather overcome.

"Precisely," said Clotilde gaily. "He is shrewd, he is smart, he knows how to manage people! He has the gift for intrigue which is indispensable to a statesman! He adores women, and we adore him! I have, for years. I admit it!"

Rosalind resolved to take the advice of the

kind, worldly woman, and followed her discreet suggestions to the letter. She set the table with the finest china, plus an array of the most silver she had ever set out, a low epergne filled with costly autumn flowers of the prettiest hues of crimson, gold, orange, and yellow. Silver tea sets, silver vases of more flowers about the dining room and drawing rooms. She found gifts for each guest, silver pomade jars for the men and golden rouge pots for the ladies, and wrapped them in silver paper, to set at each place.

When it was about time for the guests to arrive, she was ready in her new crimson and scarlet and orange dress, of filmy chiffon shading in hues from the brilliant colors about her throat, to lighter at the waist, to layers of chiffon skirts, to the palest hues at her slim ankles. Clotilde had arrived early, to direct the dressing of Rosalind's hair, loose and flowing, tied with a scarlet ribbon, which made her look both young and sophisticated at one time. The ribbon was threaded skillfully through the long brown curls.

She wore scarlet shoes, with high heels of gold which glittered when she walked. Her only jewelry besides her engagement and wedding rings was a gold chain with a huge glowing topaz at the throat. Norah beamed at her charge in great delight.

"Ye will be the finest lady there. Now ye look as ye should—a fine, beautiful lady!" Norah raved.

"You are correct!" Clotilde herself wore her favorite emerald green, in a shining silk and satin taffeta fabric, with emeralds at her ears and throat and on her white, bare arms. "Now, we shall descend! Head up proudly, my dear!" She put a golden fan in Rosalind's hand and pronounced her ready.

The two ladies descended the stairs together. Rosalind was intensely aware of the men waiting below for them, her father, Adam, Fritz, and Warynski. They were waiting in the hallway, heads upturned. She glanced at her father, saw the wonder and pride in his look, and could almost forgive him for what he had done in his blundering love for her.

She could not look at Adam. But her husband stepped forward, took her hand, kissed the wrist, then greeted Madame Denhof in the same way, thanking her for arranging the meeting.

"Poof! It is nothing! Clément is a darling," she said gaily. "He adores dinner parties, and he adores me! It was simple!"

"Simple! When we have tried to reach him—for months!" said Warynski rather grimly.

Adam said low, in Rosalind's ear, near his shoulder, "Is this the crimson gown she instructed you to wear?"

She nodded, not daring to glance up at him. She did not want to see cool indifference, or, worse, to have him pretend interest in her.

"You are stunningly beautiful, my dear," he said. She caught her breath.

"Th-thank you," she said, and moved forward nervously as the butler opened the front door to the first guests. The evening went then in the speed of light, people coming until they seemed to fill the huge rooms.

She led Prince Metternich in to dinner, and found him as Clotilde had said. She had ignored a few social rules and set Madame Denhof on his other side, and found it a smart gesture. He had much in common with her friend, and they kept up an easy conversation. Clément Metternich did dearly love to talk, Rosalind found, and a few smiles, glances of deepest interest at him when he made profound remarks, would encourage him to talk on and on.

She was much aware of the malicious interest of Isabelle de Guise in the center of the table, and her brother, Jerome, near her. Their eyes were sparkling; they were always whispering to neighbors and laughing. She wished she had not invited them, but Clotilde had ordered it, as they were friends of Metternich.

The Polish dishes were received with great interest. She had decided to begin with a vegetable soup enriched with sour cream, which they pronounced delicious. Then a fish course, of a local variety. This was followed by a mixed grill of Polish sausage, deer, veal, and pork, with some sour and spicy sauces to add as each guest wished.

The meal concluded with one of the elaborate decorative sugar pieces, a huge cake crowned with flowers and birds in richest icing. The Hungarian wines were set with each course, white wines to begin, then creamy white with the fish, and a fine red wine with the meats.

She tasted nothing. She ate something of the

foods on her plate, but was more concerned that the conversation should flow, that she could tactfully speak of Poland to Metternich.

"Yes, yes, the matter goes badly," he said once, to Clotilde's questioning. "Some men can be so stubborn!"

It did not sound good, Rosalind thought, and met the flashing sparkle of Clotilde's green eyes. The woman adored a challenge!

She led the ladies to the drawing room following dinner, and was just beginning to serve coffee to them when the gentlemen, led by Adam, walked in. His face was grave. Metternich was not with them.

Rosalind gazed up at him. Isabelle de Guise, stunning in a deep-blue dress of gauze, cut low to show her white bosom, was standing near Rosalind's coffee table.

"Has the guest of honor left so early?" said the French woman in a clear, ringing tone. Her laughter chimed; her eyes were not laughing. "How humiliating! Perhaps he became ill on all that rich Polish food!"

"I am sure not," said Adam in his deliberately calm tone. "He had a meeting this evening. He apologized for leaving so hurriedly, Rosalind. He will write you a note. He had not realized the hour was so late, he had enjoyed his conversation with you so much!"

"Thank you, sir," she said stiffly, worried for him, concerned about Metternich. Her hand trembled when she lifted a cup, and the china clattered. Isabelle's sharp eyes missed nothing.

"What a disaster," said the girl as her brother strolled up to join them. "Jerome, just think. Metternich has walked out, without taking leave of his so charming hostess!"

"And how beautiful she does look this evening," said her brother, his eyes on the low bosom of the crimson dress. "The butterfly has emerged from the pale English muslins, eh? Vienna has done much for you, Countess!"

Rosalind's color was deepening at the malicious tones of the brother and sister. She was distressed for Adam, worried about the implications of Metternich's leaving.

"It is too bad," said Isabelle de Guise, "that she will not be in Vienna long enough to become cosmopolitan! It takes more than money and a good chef to entertain Prince Metternich! Were you able to speak more than two words to him, Countess?" There was a strong, sneering emphasis on Rosalind's title.

Truly, she had spoken little to the Prince. He seemed not to need conversation, he could carry on a fine monologue. But she could not say that. She looked down helplessly at the coffee cup, and wondered if she could pour a drop without spilling it.

"I think you did not know that *my wife* has been hostess for her father in London society for some years, since her childhood, in fact," said Adam smoothly, with a hard edge to his tone. "She is no green hostess. Her taste is excellent. And her intelligence is most unusual. It is not every lady who can converse fluently in five languages, would you say, de Guise?"

Rosalind was close to fainting. She had been attacked—and Adam himself was defending her, in terms quite unmistakable! She was unutterably grateful to him. The Frenchman laughed and answered something. They all strolled away, leaving her to tend to her duties.

When she was free, temporarily, of pouring coffee, she glanced across at Adam, in his favorite pose, leaning against the mantel, his lean, thoughtful face unsmiling as he listened to the chatter of an Austrian. He was ever courteous, ever polite, thought his wife, no matter how disappointed he might be.

She wished he were not disappointed in her! Even though he had married her without loving her, might she be able to win his love? It was a daring new thought, and she tested it a little breathlessly as she studied his face.

Or at least his approval. If she could work hard, dress well, help him in his cause—might she not win his approval? She could try, she thought. She could try—very hard. Because it was well worth the trying.

She loved him so hopelessly, so completely. She did not want to lose him. Would it be possible to endear herself to him in some way, so he would not leave her when the maddeningly strange Congress of Vienna came to its close?

Chapter 8

Clotilde came again the following afternoon, full of plans and intrigues. "I have not been so amused for years," she bubbled, her green eyes shining. "We shall ride on the lanes about the Prater, we shall sit in cafés, we shall plot and whisper and manage, shall we not, Rosalind?"

"I don't know," said Rosalind helplessly. "What can I do? I know so little about diplomacy and politics!"

"All the better! Men love a helpless little lady looking up at them adoringly as they expound. Excellent! Say little, but twitter with admiration at every remark!" She giggled in delight. "Now hurry, we shall go out for a drive in the Prater this afternoon! I mean to encounter Prince Metternich if we can, and demand he come again to dinner!"

"Oh, Clotilde! Do you think he would? He was not bored?"

"Never. You listened to him admirably! He thinks you are a very intelligent woman, because you scarcely opened your lips, and listened to him!" She laughed again, her eyes affectionate. "Now, what shall you wear? I am wearing my black, with plumes. I think—yes, you shall wear ruby red! We shall be stunning together!"

Still Rosalind hesitated. "I do have guests coming for tea at four . . ."

"We shall return in time. But what matter if we are late? Your husband will be so pleased if we meet Clément and make further arrangements. Come, come! Change quickly! Yes, that ruby dress, Norah!" And she hustled Rosalind into the flattering velvet dress with matching cloak and the wide-brimmed, demure bonnet of cream with ruby ribbons.

They went out in the carriage to drive along the wide avenues of the Prater, to bow in return to the gallant greetings of the many gentlemen, and to smile at the ladies in their own carriages. Clotilde kept up an amusing cynical chatter which made Rosalind laugh.

"La! How pretty your face is when you smile, Rosalind," her friend commented. "You are quite lovely. Now, he is a great friend of Talleyrand, bow to him, smile. That is right! Ah, good afternoon, Count! I am quite cross with you—you did not dance more than twice with me the other evening!" Clotilde called across to a gentleman on horseback, who came to canter at their side and exchange badinage with her.

They returned late to tea, but even her father smiled when Clotilde came in with her and enlivened their little group.

The next morning Clotilde arrived early, and insisted that Rosalind accompany her to the dressmaker's where they ordered what seemed an incredible number of dresses. "For you must be very smartly gowned from now on," said Clotilde gaily. "I shall throw away all of those pale blues and pinks which are dreadful, quite dreadful for you! You may wear only what I decree!"

"But Clotilde—those clothes—the colors . . ." Rosalind protested rather feebly. The flame colors, the brilliant oranges and scarlets and rose, all were so flattering that she could not retire into the background.

"And that dreadful gray dress! I shall burn it!" said her friend. "Horrible! I should feel quite seventy years old, should I wear it! Never again, pray, dearest! Now, what about another riding habit, one of orange and black, with orange plumes?"

"Is it—the style?" murmured Rosalind, fingering the orange velvet longingly.

"You shall make your own style," said Clotilde. "I do!"

And so, under her friend's influence, and with her strong encouragement, Rosalind began to blossom out into a vivid, unusual personality, in bright dresses which flattered her strong coloring rather than dulled it. She felt more herself, yet shy with it all, for in the drab dresses she had felt more retiring and more at ease.

And each afternoon they went for a drive in the Prater in Rosalind's smart carriage, or in Clotilde's older but distinguished one, with a crest on it. They were noticed; Clotilde saw to that. They always wore matching or contrasting clothing, to complement each other, and the gentlemen began to flock about them.

And three days later, they met Clément Metternich on their drive. He came up to them, and Clotilde ordered her coachman to halt.

"Clément! Naughty boy," she scolded the distinguished man gaily, and his wigged white head nodded at her as he beamed. "You have neglected me! How can you? You have ignored my notes?"

"Not at all, dearest." He came up, kissed her hand devotedly, turned to Rosalind, kissed her hand. As other carriages drove by, very, very slowly, Rosalind knew they were being keenly observed, jealously regarded, as they talked to the Prince. "I have been composing a letter to you for three days!"

"I much more enjoy talking to you, Clément," said Clotilde, with a subtle change in her tone, a softness, an intimacy which made Rosalind blush. "We scarcely ever have the chance to talk. . . ."

She chatted with him, teased him, and finally won his promise to come to dinner at Rosalind's on Thursday evening.

"And this time you shall not run away after dinner! I will not hear of a meeting!" And she playfully tapped his cheek with her fan.

After he had left them, Clotilde ordered the coachman to drive on. Leaning back in the carriage, she sighed. "There, he can be so difficult! But he will come now, and he will remain to talk to Adam! It may do no good, but it may do much good! We shall hope, eh?"

"Oh—yes, so much! Thank you, Clotilde! I cannot express how grateful I am to you—"

Clotilde patted her hand. "You may thank me in another way," she said, with her disarming frankness. "I wish to come to England, perhaps next spring. Will you invite me to your home in

London? I should like an entrée there! Yes?"

"Oh, yes, of course!" Rosalind was rather stunned, but grateful that she could thank her friend in a practical way. She disliked being under complete obligation to anyone, and if this was what Clotilde wanted, she should have it.

They were extremely late returning to tea. Rosalind came into the hallway with Clotilde, to find Adam pacing about, frowning a little. His face relaxed when she entered; he came to her at once and lifted her hand to kiss it.

"There you are, I was growing concerned. It is almost dark outside, Rosalind! Had you forgotten our guests?" He studied her gravely.

"I am s-s-so s-sorry," she began to stammer nervously, when Clotilde interrupted, giving her own cloak to a footman.

"You will forgive us when you hear our news," said the sophisticated woman happily. "Prince Metternich dines with you again on Thursday evening, and this time he shall not have a meeting afterwards! He promised to remain for the evening!"

Adam stared at Clotilde, then at Rosalind. He had gone rather pale. "He—the Prince—comes—again?" he asked, very slowly.

"Yes, and to talk with you, Adam. We met him in the Prater as we rode in Clotilde's carriage." Rosalind was weary, windblown, but happy. "Are—are you pleased?"

"Pleased? I cannot—believe— My God, Rosalind! It means—it must mean that he is interested— I have tried— Oh, God," he uttered, inco-

herently, and said something in Polish rapidly to
Clotilde. She laughed as she answered him.

Rosalind was learning Polish, but she could not
catch what they said. She did catch her own
name. But it meant more that Adam was gazing
at her with incredulous delight, with growing
hope and happiness.

This time the dinner was easier to plan. She
mixed Polish and Austrian dishes, had flowers arranged in low porcelain bowls set about the room
and on the long table, and invited only a dozen
guests, reluctantly including Isabelle de Guise and
her brother.

The dinner went fabulously well. Isabelle made
no catty remarks; indeed, Rosalind felt somewhat
uneasy as Isabelle and her brother treated her
with more elaborate courtesy. Whenever she met
the speculative black gaze of Isabelle, or the intense gaze of Jerome, Rosalind flinched. They
seemed to be studying her as though she were
some new creature on their horizon.

She had worn the gold tissue silk, cut low over
the bosom, with rubies set in gold for her neck-
lace and bracelet and rings. Clotilde had directed
Norah to set her hair in an elaborate swathing of
brown silky waves, crowned with a small golden
tiara.

"The butterfly has emerged from the cocoon,"
said Fritz Dabrowski in her ear, before dinner. "I
have never seen you look so radiant, my dear!
You were pretty before, now you are radiant!
Beautiful! A fit wife for Adam!"

She smiled rather tremulously before his elaborate compliments. She did not really care what anyone in the world thought of her but Adam, and his attention tonight was on Clément Metternich.

Best of all, during the evening Metternich retired to Adam's study with him and Hubert Warynski. They were gone more than an hour. Rosalind, nervously awaiting their return, made conversation with Jerome de Guise, who seemed rather devoted to her that evening, and kept leaning over her.

"Yes, I think Vienna has quite brought you out. You enjoy the plays, the concerts?" he kept asking her, his black eyes studying her face, her throat, her white bosom where it met the gold silk of the gown.

"Very much, whenever we are able to attend. Adam is quite busy," she said, with reserve.

"But then we must see that you go anyway! Shall we not, Isabelle?" he asked his sister with a smile. "What about tomorrow evening? Shall I call for you about eight?"

Rosalind stiffened. He took too much for granted! "I do not care to go about without Adam," she said, quite simply and truthfully.

"But you drive in the Prater with Madame Denhof!" said Isabelle, her eyebrows raised. "And you seem to enjoy the masculine attentions you are receiving. Of course, you are not accustomed to such flattery, are you?"

"No, I am not," said Rosalind. "I do not think I care for—flattery, anyway." And her eyes met Isabelle's bravely.

Clotilde Denhof and Fritz Dabrowski strolled near and took part in the conversation, and it became general. Rosalind thought that her friends had noticed her unease with the de Guise brother and sister, and had come deliberately.

Clotilde said later it was true. "Besides, my dearest, I do not trust them. They would make mischief if they can, I believe! You must have a care of them. I think when Clément comes again, we shall not invite the de Guises. There is too much malice in them."

"I think so also." Rosalind sighed. "But she is so very beautiful!"

Clotilde shrugged eloquently, flinging out her beautiful hands. "Beauty? What is it? What does it matter, besides the heart and mind and soul? A beauty, one wearies of that. But the mind—ah, that is quite another matter! It lasts longer, and satisfies much more!"

Rosalind thought, yes, but some men notice only the beauty! "What did you think about the fête, Clotilde?" They had mentioned the idea on a recent drive in the Prater.

Clotilde was at once distracted to the new conversation. "But of course! Your gardens are glorious, they are large. What better indeed for an entertainment? I think one might have two or three hundred persons!"

"Two or three—hundred?" asked Rosalind faintly.

"But of course! An afternoon fête, when the weather is sunny, as it often is in late October. It will not dare to rain," said Clotilde with blithe confidence.

Rosalind finally went to her father with her plans and worries. She dared not bother Adam. He was closeted most of the days with his Polish friends, or out calling on various important men. The talk with Metternich had made his hopes soar high, and they were busily evolving various plans of new borders, a new constitution for Poland, the form of government it might take, and so on.

Her father was jubilant about the event; his daughter was a great success, he declared over and over. "And why not a garden fête? All men and women are children at heart! Look at the success of the parks here, the Prater! You could have puppet shows, dances, a band, entertainments—"

He was full of ideas, and plans for carrying them out. She turned over to him the burden of planning the lighting for the gardens, the tents to be set up in case of rain (she was not so optimistic as Clotilde). Barnaby Malloy adored planning big projects—it was what had made him an immense business success—and he turned to it with gusto.

Lady Sophia Eardley and several other ladies came willingly to assist in sending out the invitations. They wrote and wrote, and Rosalind had the immense satisfaction of knowing that over four hundred guests were arriving, accepting her invitations. The day when the Russian aide arrived in a gilded carriage, bearing the acceptance of the Czar Alexander, was a day she was never to forget.

Her father fairly boiled over with excitement. Adam was quite pale and excited, as she had never seen him. Clotilde beamed and beamed, and could not quite conceal the little-girl pleasure under her sophistication.

They had had scarcely little more than a week to plan it. It must be crushed into a day between a Russian fireworks and music demonstration and an Austrian equestrian parade. But they managed.

And Clotilde had decreed that Polish music must be played and the dances must be mostly Polish. So there must be rehearsals. Rosalind knew the polonaise, of course; it was played frequently at the balls she had attended. But Clotilde must polish the steps, the hand movements, the graceful gestures which accompanied the dance.

And she must learn thoroughly the lively mazurka, the mad oberek, the krakowiak with its spirited movements. Clotilde went over and over the dances with her, with Sophia and the other women.

On the day after the Russian Czar's acceptance of the invitation, Rosalind was practicing with the other ladies in one of the back drawing rooms.

The door was flung open, and Fritz stood there. Behind him was Adam, staring at them all as they bowed gracefully to their dance mistress, Clotilde Denhof.

"There, Adam, I told you I heard music!" said Fritz in triumph. "The ladies are dancing!"

"We—we are p—practicing the P—Polish dances," stammered Rosalind. The presence of Adam, so stern and serious, always had this effect of making her feel like a little child again, worried for fear she had acted in an unladylike manner.

"But why not in the ballroom?" he asked simply, and began to smile. "Come. Fritz and I shall lead you in the dances! And is not Sir Percy about? I saw him cooling his heels in the library, waiting for his sister! He shall also learn!"

"Percy hates to learn dances," said his sister wisely. "He likes to dance, but he doesn't like to learn!"

But Percy was brought, and did not seem very unwilling, especially when a lovely blonde girl was his partner. Fritz and Adam partnered them all in turn, but Adam spent most of his time with Rosalind, to her shy delight.

"I am pleased you wish to learn our dances," he said once, as he guided her in a mazurka. "There—that way, and lift your hand—so. You are naturally most graceful! What shall you wear to the fête?"

She caught her breath. Clotilde had found a Polish costume for her to wear, in a bright red and green and white design, with an apron of white lace. She told him shyly, anxiously, watching for his reaction.

He gazed down at her, and his dark eyes sparkled. "So—you shall indeed look like a Polish girl," he said, with obvious pleasure. "And your long lovely hair in braids, no?"

"Clotilde said I should."

"Excellent!"

Adam and Fritz remained with them until teatime, when the ladies relaxed over the cups. They departed then for a meeting, but the glow of Adam's approval remained with Rosalind. She wanted so much to make him happy!

Chapter 9

"That fête," exclaimed Barnaby Malloy, "was a smashing success, it was!"

And it really was, from beginning to end. The sun shone on the cool November day as if to bless the event, Vienna, and all who lived there. People began arriving in the late morning, headed for the tables laden with food and the kegs of cold beer, and ate as though they had not eaten for months.

All three chefs had worked for a week on preparations. There were Polish hams and Austrian veal and British beef, mutton, and venison, and jellied dishes. There was cold borscht, thick and purple with beets. Cabbage soup. Thick soups with sour cream. And fish, in cold and hot dishes; chicken, goose, duck, rabbit, pheasant, and plates and platters of hot smoked Polish sausage. There were sauces both sweet and sour for every dish.

And there were the plates and tables of other foods—the beans and mushrooms and beets and gherkins and cucumbers. Breads of wheat and rye, dumplings, pancakes rolled with jelly. Apples, plums, pears, imported grapes piled in purple heaps.

For dessert there were honeyed sweet buns, chocolate tortes in seven layers of richness, white cakes and yellow cakes and spice cakes with caramel icing. There were tarts with strawberries, some with cherries, some with chocolate, all heaped with snowy whipped cream. And the huge cake, of nine layers, as big as a wedding cake, with a map of Poland on the top!

Families with children came early to watch the puppet shows, laughing at the merry pranks. They sat to watch the magicians, romped about the merry-go-round (Barnaby's special pride), or went over to the nearby meadow to ride the small Shetland ponies Barnaby had discovered somewhere. Besides the formal entertainment, there was always someone to organize a game of ball or hide-and-seek.

People came and went, the carriages rolled up and away again. Some came on horseback—whole families of them—complaining merrily of the thick traffic on the roads to their residence. "It is like the Prater on a Sunday," declared more than one matron, attempting to gather her children together again to get them to depart.

Barnaby Malloy had arranged a small dance floor in one corner of the gardens. There a band played most of the time, and most of the airs were Polish. Adam came to Rosalind early in the afternoon, where she was busily meeting guests, directing them to various amusements.

"You must come with me," he said in a low, urgent tone.

"Oh—Adam, is something wrong?"

"You will see," he said quietly. She gazed up at him anxiously, then went with him, skipping along in her red Polish boots, which showed her slim legs to mid-calf. Her red and green and white skirts swung as they clasped hands and walked along the grass. Adam bowed low to several guests as they went, but he did not pause.

They went directly to the band, and Adam said, "Now play the waltz for me."

And with a rare smile, he swung Rosalind into the dance. "The first waltz. Rosalind," he reminded her. They were the only ones on the floor at first.

"Oh—Adam—I thought something was wrong," she gasped, as she realized he had brought her all the way over there for a dance! Her heart seemed to be jumping about crazily.

"Something is wrong," he said calmly. "I have scarcely seen you for weeks!" And he drew her closer, his arm about her slim waist.

He was wearing his Polish cavalry uniform, and had added several of the decorations from among the many he was entitled to wear. He had never looked so handsome and fine, she thought fondly, gazing at him. Oh, if only—if only—

The waltz was over all too soon. She returned to her guests, and Adam walked about among them

also, greeting them informally, making them welcome. Later in the afternoon she saw Czar
Alexander talking to Adam jovially, slapping his
back, clasping his arm. She wondered if they
were talking politics, or women. Still later, she
saw the Czar standing watching the puppet show,
fascinated as a child, with a beautiful, sophisticated princess on each arm!

What a mixture he is, she thought, the young
dynamic head of the vast Russian Empire. He
was said to have high ideals, ambitious ideas for
the people, and yet he spent much of his time, ac-
cording to gossips, in the bedrooms of lovely
women who spoiled and flattered him. She
studied his handsome face, puzzled. She wondered how much he would have to say about the
future of Adam's beloved Poland.

Clément Metternich arrived late in the afternoon, escorting a current lovely. He bowed his
powdered white head again and again, bowed before ladies, kissed Rosalind's hand, flattered her
about the fête in ponderous, endless prose, and
seemed genuinely delighted to have come.

Barnaby Malloy dashed from one of his enter-
prises to another. When the merry-go-round
threatened to break down, he took off his coat,
rolled up his sleeves, and had the works going
again in a trice. Then he went over to see about
the ponies, and again to observe the balloons, that
there might be more than enough for everyone.
But the fireworks scheduled for the end of the
fête, just at dusk, were his pride, his joy, and his
anxiety. He went again and again to the work-

men, scolding them, advising them, telling them just how to set them off and in what order.

Prince Metternich came to Rosalind presently, with the air of one well fed. She had observed him drinking the Hungarian wines thirstily, and becoming even more animated.

"My dearest Countess, you must dance the polonaise with me!" he declared. "I have been waiting the afternoon to dance with you!"

Barnaby Malloy was near enough to hear him, and his pride in his daughter threatened to burst his waistcoat. He a tradesman, and his daughter was being asked by a potent prince of Europe for the honor of her hand in a dance! He followed them at a discreet distance, and beamed at Rosalind when she glanced over her shoulder at him and smiled.

Clotilde Denhof also observed them, and was quick to seize the attention of Czar Alexander, to beg him to join the dance. Adam came up and sought Lady Sophia Eardley in the dance. And so they began, at Adam's direction, and Rosalind led the polonaise with Prince Metternich as her gracious partner. She was in a dream of delight. Adam seemed so happy, the Prince was cordial, Alexander was gracious; all seemed to be going so very well.

And the fête—more than four hundred had come, she was assured by the butler, who had been meticulously counting and making notes for her. But the food and drink were ample, and guests came and went all the day.

Rosalind tried to keep an eye on the tables. But

she did not need to worry. The chefs were keeping up a friendly rivalry to see who could supply the most dishes, whose were the most popular, and they saw to it that the maids went scurrying back and forth, to and from the kitchens, with fresh hot and cold dishes. The ices were a great success, in lemon and lime and strawberry flavors, rivaling the pretty tarts in favor.

All too soon, it began to grow dark. Barnaby Malloy gave the signal, and the fireworks began to shoot into the air, in patterns of stars and flowers, and a final grand flag of Poland.

As they watched, Rosalind was aware that Adam had left her side. Then he returned, putting a crimson velvet cloak about her shoulders.

"You will be chilly here in the night air, my dear," he said simply.

Her heart seemed to overflow with joy. That Adam should be so concerned for her! It was the final crowning touch to a perfect day. She felt his hand slip onto her arm under the cloak, as the fireworks blazed, white and crimson, green and blue, accompanied by "oohs" and "aahhs" from the crowd.

When the fireworks ended, she and Adam went to the entrance of the gardens, to bid the guests good-bye. The carriages were jammed near the entrances, and it took more than an hour and a half to load the passengers. But it was finally over, and the hosts went inside, to stretch their weary limbs on couches and chairs, and relive the fête once again.

"Ah, went well, I think," said Barnaby.

"Well? It was glorious!" said Fritz spontaneously. "Grandest occasion yet. And everyone here, Alexander and Metternich, and Lord Castlereagh came for a bit this afternoon. And Talleyrand dropped in at luncheon. And the German princes, I counted five of them!"

"Does anyone want any dinner?" asked Rosalind wearily. She herself was so full of food and excitement, she could not bear to think of eating.

They all heard the voices on the veranda, and sat up straight, staring at each other in amazement. Clotilde Denhof came casually into the room by the French windows, on the arm of Clément Metternich! They were talking animatedly, then paused as they met the concerted stares of their hosts.

"Oh—we have not left," said Clotilde, with an enchanting smile, but underneath she seemed rather serious and pensive, thought Rosalind. "We have something—to discuss."

Adam had risen at once, to greet them courteously, covering his surprise.

"I shall order tea—or dinner," said Rosalind, at once.

"No, not for me, nothing, please," said the Prince, seriously. "Ah—I must leave presently. But I wished to speak privately with you, Count Potocki, and with your lovely Countess."

"But of course!" said Adam. Rosalind could only stare, speechless. It was Adam who ordered tea for the rest, asked Clotilde to pour and see to their comfort, and swept herself and the Prince into his study.

She could not imagine what Prince Metternich would have to say to them both. She had not talked politics to him, only listened as he spoke on various matters. Why had he not asked Adam alone, or Adam and Fritz?

Adam seated them in the study, and then sat down at his desk, his face looking rather pale and tense. For once the Prince seemed at a loss for words. He studied his well-manicured fingertips and cleared his throat ominously. Finally he began.

"I have become fond of you both," he said quietly, without his usual long, prosy sentences. His handsome face was, as always, in sharp contrast to the harsh nasal voice in which he spoke fluently in German, Italian, French, and even Russian. "And for that reason, I shall not bore you with false hopes, nor discourage you with doubts. I wish only to be honest with you. As I wish to be with my friends."

"I am honored—we both are honored by you," said Adam, his voice deepened. Rosalind noted how his long slim fingers had closed over a wooden box on his desk, clenching it as though he might crush it.

"Madame Denhof, whom I honor and respect, has informed me of your hopes and dreams for a united Poland. I myself know of your long career in the cavalry, your gallantry and courage. You are not a diplomat, Count Potocki. You would like to charge the enemy and win him with sheer force of arms. But that is not how it is done in the congresses—unfortunately."

Rosalind listened, fascinated, wide-eyed. Adam had flushed. "I am trying to learn the art of diplomacy," he said with dignity. "It is foreign to me. I have lived as a country man, knowing crops and animals. More recently, I served in battle. I can learn yet again—"

"I do not doubt it! Nevertheless, you are too trusting by half," said Metternich dryly. "Some you count as your friends are not friends. I say no more of that, but be warned! I came on another matter."

Rosalind scarcely heard his next words. Who were the false friends? Surely not Fritz—not Hubert Warynski.

"The Polish settlement is going badly. I had hoped to be able to carve out a new Polish state, oh, perhaps not so large as before, but nevertheless a state where the Poles might unite once more with a country and a homeland of their own. We have negotiated with the German princes and found that it might be arranged—with concessions."

"Some of them are favorable to our cause," said Adam.

"Yes. With the hope of gaining other lands! They are greedy, make no mistake about it! Well, that is not the problem now. Alexander came to the Congress with fixed ideas about Poland. The Czar has high ideals," said Metternich dryly, with a wry little smile. "I think you know what he wishes."

"I wish you would tell me in your own words," Adam said, so quietly that Rosalind might have thought him almost disinterested, except that she had noted his long slim fingers were crushing the wooden box.

"He wishes to set up an independent Polish state. He wants to furnish the Poles with a liberal constitution. But he wants all under his own thumb." And Metternich lifted his own hand, his thumb pressed downward into the other palm significantly.

Both of them gazed fascinated as the big thumb pushed at the palm. Then Metternich raised his hands, raised his shoulders in a shrug.

"Yes, under his own and Russia's rule. We cannot have this. He would be at our own borders, with an army under his command. He would lie at the gates of the German states. No, no, this is unendurable. You see?"

"Yes—I see." Adam was biting his lips, controlling his strong emotions. "But what of poor Poland? Does she not count at all? Do our wishes, our hopes, our dreams—" The words burst out of his agonized heart.

"Gently, gently, friend! The settlements have not been made! The Congress will draw on for a long time," and Metternich sighed and shook his head. "We are far apart. There is much to discuss. We wish a balanced Europe, a balanced power structure, so that what has happened the past two dozen years cannot happen again. No man such as Napoleon must be permitted to torment the peoples of Europe, to rip apart the states—that agony must never be inflicted again! No, no, there is much to negotiate." And he was off on his long prosy statements, rambling round and round in his nasal voice, uttering long, detailed, yet vague predictions of what might happen.

Rosalind wanted to slip away, to mourn quietly in private. But she would not leave Adam, not with that white line about his mouth as he listened in silence, not with that tormented look about his eyes. At least she could share his agony.

Finally Metternich drew to a close, and got up to depart. Adam stood at once, and both of them escorted the Prince to the door, where his carriage and coachmen waited patiently. The house was quiet. Rosalind realized with a start that they had been closeted with the Prince more than two hours. The guests had departed, even Clotilde.

Rosalind returned to the drawing room after the Prince's carriage had drawn away. No one was there, not even her father. Adam followed her into the room, and looked about in a dazed fashion.

"All our hopes," he muttered. "All our hopes . . ."

He was intensely weary and depressed and Rosalind could think of nothing to do but order tea. She rang for the footman and ordered it quietly.

Adam had sunk down on a couch and was bent over, his face in his hands. He kept rubbing his fingers restlessly over the red scar on his cheek as though it hurt him.

Tea was brought, and small sandwiches of meat and cheese. She filled his cup, took it to him. He shook his head as though he did not see her, as though she were some small irritation he could shake off.

"Adam, have some tea and eat something," she urged gently. "You know this is not the end. Clotilde told me the negotiations might drag on for months. This is only the beginning."

"The beginning—my God," he said fervently, and crossed himself. "Oh, my God, Rosalind—what are we to do?"

"Keep on fighting," she said, simply. "The cause is not lost. Did you ever win a battle in the first skirmishes?" She studied his raised face anxiously, hoping she could reach him.

Unexpectedly his face lightened, his brows raised at her words. "The battles—God, no. Of course not. I should have thought—no, of course they are not won so fast. And this is the most difficult battle I have ever tried to fight! He was right, Rosalind, I am no diplomat!" The words rang bitterly.

"Drink your tea, Adam," she ordered, and was surprised when he lifted the teacup to his lips automatically, like an obedient child, and began to drink. She put a small sandwich into his hands. "Eat, Adam, please. This will help. Tomorrow you can think more clearly. Tomorrow—there is always tomorrow, God willing."

"Yes—yes—God willing," he said, with a heavy sigh, and began to eat.

Chapter 10

Rosalind retired to her rooms, but found she was quite unable to sleep. She put on her golden night robe and matching negligee, said her prayers, and climbed into bed, but the events of the day swirled round and round in her brain.

Finally she got up, went into her sitting room, and looked for a book to read. She must think of something else, to get her mind off the future.

But the book could not hold her attention. She paced about, opened the window, and closed it again, for the night wind was quite chilly. She poked up the fire, and stood to warm her cold hands at it.

The tap on the door startled her. "Who is it?" she called.

The door to Adam's rooms opened abruptly, and Adam came in. He, too, was dressed for the night, in robe and slippers. He seemed pale and drawn.

"I heard you stirring about and thought you could not sleep either," he said. "May I talk to you for a time?"

"Of course, Adam. I—I have been thinking—and trying to stop thinking," she said, with a ghost of a smile. "I'll prod the fire a bit; it is reluctant to start." And she picked up the poker once more.

"Let me." He came over and took the poker

from her, touching her hand lightly as he did so. "You are cold! Is there a blanket—a rug you might put over you?"

"Yes, I'll get one." She went to the bedroom and returned with a crimson blanket. She sat down on the couch and put it over her knees, curling up thankfully under it. Adam was poking the fire with vigorous skill, making it blaze. Finally he set the poker down and came to sit in a chair near her couch.

He leaned forward, his elbows on his knees, gazing into the fire. After a time, he said wearily, "This has been much more of a shock. I had begun to hope once more. Prince Metternich seemed so interested. Now— this blow, I am sure he would not lie to us, he is telling the truth."

"Yes, he is honest. But, Adam, are there not ups and downs in any such matter? Perhaps this week the situation looks desperate. Next week—who knows? Someone may give way in his position; there may be other concerns."

"Yes, I have said that to myself, Rosalind. But consider. Alexander of Russia has not changed his position by an iota in the weeks and months he has been in Vienna. Not a bit. He is a stubborn man, and a powerful one. He might win his way."

"That is possible," she said quietly, studying Adam's face with deep compassion and concern. She had never seen him so depressed. Of course, he was tired. It had been a very busy day, and he had been working hard for weeks before it.

She herself was so weary that every bone seemed to ache. She shifted her position against the cushions, and under the rug she rubbed her ankles. She had stood, and danced, and walked, and stood some more for hours and hours that day.

Once he had begun, Adam seemed unable to stop talking. He spoke of his hopes, his concerns. He told her how they had begun writing a new constitution for Poland, how it might be organized once Poland was free again. Feverishly he spoke of the parliament organization, the election of a head of state, how a new education policy might be set up, the freedom of the lower classes.

"It is not right that a few nobles should control the lives of many underlings. I have seen men fight under me with no learning, no nobility. Yet they fought with devotion, with courage, with high regard for the lives of their comrades."

He rubbed the scar again and again. She longed to reach out and put her long slim hands on his cheeks, to cool his feverish head, to calm him. But he would not like it, she thought. He did not love her. He thought only of his Poland. That was why he had married her.

She leaned her head back and listened. This much she could do. He went on and on, until his weary, husky voice finally stumbled over the words. He said something in Polish, something about being tired.

"Yes, you must get some sleep," she said. "It will look better tomorrow. We are both weary, Adam. Tomorrow you will have the strength to begin once more."

"Yes. Yes, to begin once more," he muttered.

He stood, to pace restlessly across the drawing room, and came back to stand behind her near the end of the couch. "Thank you, Rosalind. You have listened very kindly to me. You are a most generous person," he said, and the words, in his deep tones, moved her deeply.

"I wish—I wish—to make things well for you," she stammered awkwardly. "I only wish I could do—d-do much m-more. It might be possible to have a dinner for the Czar—"

She started nervously when his hand descended to her shoulder, and held it so firmly that she felt his warmth through the two layers of gold silk. She stiffened, and tried to shift away from his hand.

"You have helped immeasurably, just by being here—your presence, your graciousness," he said, she thought, rather formally. "You are a most experienced hostess, you make all your guests feel welcome and at home. My mother has commented on this."

"I am glad—she is pleased. She is a dear," said Rosalind, wondering if his mother had spoken to Adam about her wish for him to have a son! Somehow, in her weariness, the thought was distasteful. She did not want Adam pushed into intimacies he did not really want.

His hand moved slightly, and caressed her neck. She jumped visibly. His fingers were slim, hard, yet gentle. They sent a tingle down her spine, made her shiver even under the robe.

"The marriage was rather sudden, we have scarcely had an opportunity to become acquainted.

I thought we would soon come to know each other's thoughts, but indeed we have both been much too busy. I shall be glad when this Congress business is over," he said, and sighed deeply. "It is too much of a worry. What will happen to Poland—one does not know."

Still his hand absently caressed her neck, and her shoulder. She was stiff under his touch, rather offended that he should caress her, touch her without permission. He did not really care for her, she thought. He spoke no words of tenderness, no words of love.

Probably he was too honest to speak of love when he felt none for her.

"I had thought it would be better to wait till this business was over before we married," he went on absently. His other hand touched her shoulder, and both hands went over and over her shoulders and arms. Very stiff now, and apprehensive, and tired to the point of jumpiness, she sat still, fighting to keep from yielding to him. No, she would not yield without love.

"It might have been better—to w-wait," she agreed. "We c-could have become more acquainted—and then—m-married in London—if—if we still wanted to."

His hands paused for a moment; the silence in the room seemed to stifle her.

"But you care for me a little, I think, Rosalind," he said quietly. She wished she could see his face. Did he look anxious, or triumphant? Did he know she loved him, adored him, though he cared nothing for her? Was this a sop to her vanity, to her feelings, so that she might continue working hard for him, encouraging her father to give him more money?

The thought was intensely distasteful to her, humiliating, and degrading to them both. With an effort, she slid away from him, threw off the rug, and came to her feet. She flung around to face him.

"Please do not touch me like that, Adam," she said, as coldly as possible. "I d-do not like it! You do not need to feel that—that you must—I mean . . ." She faltered as she saw the intense look in his eyes. What did he mean, looking at her like that? As though he saw through her to her very heart?

He came around the couch slowly toward her, put one hand on her waist easily, and drew her toward him. She was pressed close to his body before she knew it. He put his other hand to the back of her mussed dark curls, and held her face beneath his. His head bent.

She tried to turn her head, frantically, at the last moment, as she saw his purpose. "No—do not—Adam—do not—" she gasped.

His large firm mouth came down on hers, and pressed warmly. Her lips were slightly open, in protest—his mouth was so warm, so close, so intimate. She had never in her life been kissed like that. As though he felt possessive, as though he took control of her, as though he wanted her—

Her very body seemed to melt limply as he held her closer. He kissed her expertly, it seemed to her inexperience. His mouth twisted against her lips, almost forcing a response, though she tried to turn her head away. He was drugging her with his sweetness, his passion. His hand on her waist, sliding lower, touched her thighs, and seemed to burn through the soft fabric of her gowns.

Why, why? she thought in agony, in weary distress. He did not love her. For a man, was the passion of the moment enough? It was not enough for her! She would not be the wife of a man who had married her only for the money!

Oh, she knew his cause was a burning fire in him, but that still did not justify his actions!

She wrenched herself away from him, nerves jumpy, feelings outraged that he should seem to conquer her so easily. No, mere passion would not satisfy her! It was not enough.

"Do not, do not!" she raged, pushing him away from her with her hands against his chest. She stiffened her elbows to keep him off, as he would have pulled her close again. He gazed down at her, his eyes bemused, dark with passion. "I will not have it—no, I will not!"

"Why not, Rosalind?" he asked simply, his grip tightening. "Have I not waited long enough? You agreed to marry me, oh, reluctantly, but you did agree. How long did you think I would wait for this?"

"You—you married me—" She began to stammer, then stopped herself. "I married you—because m-my father wanted me to do so!" she blurted out angrily. "I w-wanted to please him. But it was too hasty—we should have waited!"

His grip slackened slowly; his eyes gazing

down into hers seemed to see beyond her face, beyond her outraged glare. Finally he released her and stepped back. His face was pale again, grave, rather weary once more, after the flush of passion had died.

"You do not know what you say, Rosalind," he said rather proudly. "You are weary; I should not have approached you tonight. Let us not speak of this again tonight. Tomorrow, we shall—"

"Tomorrow, I shall feel the same way!" He had spoken no words of love. He merely wanted her to satisfy his masculine passions. For comfort, perhaps, because he was grieved over his cause. For the reasons of a man. But not for love. He could not have her for this, no matter how much she craved his embrace, his kisses.

"I thought you had come to—to like me," he said.

He had guessed that she loved him! This was his way of approaching her, of giving her something in gratitude for her help—and her father's. No, it would not do. She had waited for years to find the right man to marry, to marry for love. She had mistaken him, but her ideals would not be demeaned!

"No, I like you, Adam," she said angrily. "But that is not—not l-love! I will not be bedded because you merely want a woman! I will not!"

He gave her a strange look. His mouth curled in a slight smile which enraged her further. "Because you are a woman? Oh, Rosalind!"

She clenched her fists, for he would have reached out for her once more. "No, I mean it! Do not touch me! I am very angry with you—that you—that you—want me that way," she said incoherently.

"I would be much angrier if I did not want you that way," he said, and she had a feeling that he was laughing at her.

"*Oh!* How can you say that?" She was bewildered, flustered, furious. She glared at him like an angry cat, her head flung back. "I think—I think you do not know me! Not at all! If you think I would—that I could—"

He was grave once more, the flash of laughter gone. "Rosalind, you are very immature! I should have realized that, remembered it—"

"Immature!" she flared. "I am twenty-two!"

"And I am thirty-four. I must seem quite ancient to you! I feel ancient at times—all that I have seen, the battles, the death . . ." And she saw his hand had gone up unconsciously once more to rub at that red scar on his cheek. "But we are not so far apart at times, I think. This was the wrong night to say anything, that is true. We are both weary from the day and from the news of Metternich. Well, let us forget tonight."

"Forget it," she said blankly.

"Yes." He gave her a slight smile, and moved toward the door. "Goodnight, Rosalind. I think you drive with Clotilde in the morning?"

"Yes—at least, we had planned—"

"Very good. I will see you at luncheon, then. Good night." He paused at the door of her room, looked back at her questioningly.

"G-good night, Adam," she said. He nodded,

and opened the door and went through it. He closed it after him, and she remained gazing at that blank door for moments.

"Immature," she muttered. "Oh—immature! How dare you! I am not immature. What do you mean?"

But the blank door did not answer. She finally realized she was intensely weary, her limbs drooping and aching. She went to her bedroom and crawled into her wide, lonely bed, wanting to weep a little.

But instead, sleep overcame her at once, and she slept deeply. She dreamed Adam was holding her shoulders, and his soft caressing voice was murmuring in her ears—words of love and desire, such as she wanted to hear.

Chapter 11

They were due to spend the following evening at the rented house of the de Guises. Neither Adam nor Rosalind wanted very much to attend, but Metternich was due, and Adam wished to lose no opportunity to speak with him.

To his bitter disappointment, and to the chagrin of the hosts, Metternich sent his regrets at the last moment.

"You are more successful than I at enticing Prince Metternich to your home," smiled Isabelle de Guise, as she greeted Adam and Rosalind and gave them the news that the honored guest would not be present. "What is your secret? I must discover it."

Adam could not conceal his disappointment, and left Rosalind to answer the idle talk of their host and hostess. Jerome de Guise made himself Rosalind's escort, and insisted on showing her several of the drawing rooms of the lovely home they had rented for the Congress. She went to three of them with him, duly admired the dainty French furniture, the rare rugs and paintings. Then, finding that Adam had not come with them, she made her excuses to return to the main drawing room.

"We have neglected your other guests," she said quietly, to his protests.

"But I wanted to be alone with you!" he protested with a slight smile, watching her face alertly.

"I do not know why," she said bluntly. "I am a married woman. If you are trying to learn about politics, you waste your time with me. The intricacies are beyond me." And she turned toward the entry door.

He barred her way with a velvet-clad arm. She glanced up at the black eyes, which seemed cold and hard to her, though he was smiling. He was handsome to some, she thought; indeed, he was quite popular with some ladies. But she distrusted the cynical man, his devious ways, the cunning with which he flattered.

"Do you not know how attractive you have become, Rosalind?" he said softly. "Something has brought you out amazingly. Who would have

thought you would have become a real beauty?"
And he gazed down at the low-cut bosom of her
flame-colored dress, the rubies at her neck and on
her bare arm. His stare seemed to soil her, and
she flinched from it.

"Thank you," she said, very coldly. "Pray excuse me. I would return to the others!" And she
pushed past him. He tried to stop her, caught her
by the waist. "Sir!" she said, outraged.

"Oh, come now," he said softly. "A little kiss—
to show we are friends? No one could think that
amiss!" And he bent his head and tried to aim a
kiss at her. She struck upward with a hard palm,
caught him by the side of the head, and in the
confusion managed to slip away from him.

She went straight for the door, not pausing to
see if he followed. She went to the drawing room,
entered, and saw Adam standing near the mantel.
She went over to him and stood near him. He
paused in his speaking to another Polish friend,
and glanced down at her questioningly. She
caught a glimpse of her face in the mirror over
the ornate mantel. She was flushed, and looked
disturbed.

She composed her expression, smiled at the
gentlemen, and said something polite in answer to
the Polish greeting, allowing her hand to be cere-
monially kissed. Then she retreated to the couch
near several ladies she knew. They included her
readily in their conversation.

She resolved not to be caught alone with
Jerome de Guise. She was shrewd enough to
know he was not enamoured of her beauty. He

had some other motive for trying to catch her alone and kiss her in corners.

She saw Isabelle casting a quick glance at her, saw the cold black eyes like her brother's studying her critically. But the Frenchwoman was excessively polite to her these days, treating her with much respect, unlike her first casual dismissal. She finds me more of a formidable opponent than she had judged me, Rosalind thought, finding some satisfaction in the idea.

Isabelle soon led them in to dinner. It was a long one, with many elaborate courses. Wines followed with each course, and Rosalind soon found she must only sip at each, or her head would begin to swim alarmingly.

She noted that Adam also sipped, and then neglected his wine glass, while Jerome and Isabelle both tried to encourage his drinking. They did not know with whom they were dealing, she decided, with an inward smile. If they thought to make Adam drunken and foolish in public, they were wasting their time! He was mature, and too experienced for that. But she did wonder at their motives.

Two evenings later, they met again at a formal ball. Once more, Jerome de Guise tried to dance often with Rosalind, and once he managed to get her into the corner of an almost deserted side room.

"We have scarcely had a chance to speak together," he said intimately, putting his arm about her.

She stiffened, and put her hand decisively on

his hand. "Release me, if you please, sir," she said formidably. "I do not like these intimacies!" Her voice was loud enough to arouse the attention of an amorous couple in another corner, and they stared at Jerome and Rosalind.

His face flushed somewhat. "Do you not like me? I think you do, though you would pretend not."

"I do not pretend, sir. You mistake me if you think so," she said firmly, almost rudely. "I have few close friends. And I do not encourage such liberties. If you do not release me, I shall complain to my husband of your gross behavior!"

"Do you think he will care? The Europeans are not such sticklers for formalities as the English!" he said, with a careless laugh. "And I have heard it said that the Prince Regent has his own amusements—"

She turned on him, outraged. "Sir, you will not speak of my country and my royal family in such manner! I am furious at your daring to do so!"

He saw she was really angry, and begged her pardon in a most charming manner. "Indeed, do not be angry with me, dear lady! This is the fashion, to speak of the great ones in ways which bring them down to our level. It is the times, do you not think so? But it is indeed rude and vulgar, and I think you are too fine a lady to condone it. It is persons such as yourself, my dearest Rosalind, who keep up the tone of a company and a society. I think it is this quality in you, your fine manners and high ideals, which first drew me to you."

"Thank you, sir," she said, rather frigidly. But who could be completely cold when a handsome man of the world said such compliments in such a sincere manner?

"Please forgive me, and allow me to return you to the company in a somewhat friendly manner. I do not want to believe you are very angry with me," he coaxed, and drew her hand onto his arm, patting it as though she were a child.

She felt a little foolish, thinking later that she had threatened to report him to Adam. As though Adam would care what she did! But, on reflection, she did believe that Adam cared that his wife be a lady at all times, and not cast discredit on his name.

When they returned to the ballroom, Jerome was chatting lightly with her, bending his dark head devotedly to hers. She saw that a number of persons noted them, and whispered to each other when she returned with Jerome. She resolved that he should not catch her alone any other time, if she could prevent it.

Gossip spread like butter among the soft company that surrounded the Congress of Vienna. It would not take much talk to ruin a girl's name, and the fuel for gossip was the little sign of interest of one man in a particular lady. She herself had noted such persons at balls and at dinners, and guessed that the interest was a prelude to an affair, for to have many affairs was the manner of the day.

Adam came to claim her for a dance, and she noted that he was limping slightly.

"Adam, I think you are almost as weary as I am," she said softly, as they moved into the dance. "Would you mind very much if we were to leave early tonight? I do not think Metternich or any of the great ones will be coming."

He gazed down at her gravely. "You are rather flushed. Do you have a fever?" And he put his hand on her forehead briefly.

She flushed at his unexpected concern. "I do not believe so. I am just weary."

"It is no wonder. You work hard much of the day, and dance or go about much of the evenings with me. Yes, do let us return home early, Rosalind." And he called for their carriage to be brought.

She was glad to be sitting beside him in the closed carriage as the horses trotted through the dimly lit streets of the crisp November night. She was warmed by the carriage rug, and by his closeness. His consideration was dear to her, though she knew he did not love her.

Perhaps one day they might come to some agreement about their lives, she mused. They did get on quite well together, and his mother had a growing fondness for her. It might work—it might. Could she be satisfied with the mild attachment of her husband, his expressed appreciation for her hard work? She flinched as she compared this with the love she had thought to win someday.

It might be that some women were doomed never to be loved as they wished, that the great reservoirs of their own love had to remain dammed up and unused. Unseen in the darkness, her gloved hand crept up to her heart and pressed against it. If only it were possible to let her love for him spill over into expression!

At the doorway he handed her inside, saw her to the stairs, then said, "I think I shall work in my study for a time. Good night!"

"Good night, Adam," she said, and went up to her rooms. She had sent Norah to bed early, thinking she herself would not be home until two or three in the morning. Now she sat down in front of the low fire, and mused for a time before retiring.

The following afternoon, only three guests came to tea, and they were close friends. They were laughing and chatting idly when Adam came in from his study. Barnaby Malloy was sitting with his feet up on the fender when the footman hastened to the door and gestured frantically for Rosalind's attention.

"The carriage of His Highness Prince Metternich is approaching. Were you expecting him, Miss?" he stammered, forgetting to give her her own title in his agitation.

She felt a great rush of excitement, but managed to calm herself. "No, but we shall manage," she said calmly. She sent him back to the door, and gestured to Adam, who came over at once. "Prince Metternich is approaching," she said. "I shall order fresh tea." And she did so, a little amused at the changing expressions on Adam's usually serious face.

They went to the door to greet their unexpected guest, and found he was accompanied by Madame Denhof. Her face sparkled with her pleasure as she greeted Rosalind.

"We were driving about, darling, and then we had the impulse to call upon you! Do forgive us for not notifying you, love. Oh, the air is so fresh and marvelous today!" And she swept in, greeting Barnaby Malloy with the affection of a close friend.

The Prince was in an amiable mood, not condescending nor formal. His white-powdered head nodded and nodded as he talked and listened during tea to all they had to say to him, as he discoursed on recent events in the Congress. He ate and drank enormously of the tea, the little Austrian and Polish pastries, commenting with delight on some new cake.

Rosalind sat demurely behind the tea tray, seeing that cups were refilled. The small company was a delight, only these few close friends. Adam was able to be seated next to the Prince and converse with him informally, listening and talking gravely or lightly as they wished. Clotilde encouraged their conversation with her delightful animation and her quick, rather cynical wit.

"Well, well, I did come to talk to Count Potocki alone," said the Prince finally, seeming to realize that none of the guests could leave until he did. "Forgive us, one and all. What a delightful afternoon—my, yes, delightful! Let us retire to your study for a time, sir," he said to Adam, and the two of them went away at once.

The other three guests left, though obviously consumed by curiosity. Rosalind saw to their comfort as they left, then returned to Clotilde, who was gazing at the fire thoughtfully. Barnaby Malloy had departed also, to see to something about the horses.

"How kind you are," she said, squeezing Clotilde's hand. "Adam had just said he had not seen the Prince for such a time, and he was worried about the negotiations, yet did not wish to interfere."

Clotilde smiled. "I rather believe the news is encouraging for a change. We shall see," she said drily. "It is my experience that matters go up and down, up and down, until one is dizzy and weary of it all! The longest-lasting diplomat has the last word! How dull politics can be! I would rather intrigue in matters of love than politics! So much more satisfying, and thrilling, don't you believe, my dear?"

Rosalind grimaced, and Clotilde laughed gently. "I do not like intriguing at all," said Rosalind with a sigh.

"No, poor dear, you are too honest and direct. Tell me, what are the de Guises doing these days? I have heard an extremely odd rumor that you are enamoured of Jerome de Guise! I cannot believe your bad taste! It is incredible. Tell me all about it!"

Rosalind groaned aloud. "Oh, no, no! I feared so! I don't know why, Clotilde, but Jerome de Guise persists in following me about and attempting to kiss me. I know he cares nothing for me, and my raving beauty is *not* enough to drive a man mad! No matter how he swears that it is!" She tried to laugh.

Clotilde surveyed her gravely, shrewdly. "So— he is pursuing you, is he? That is not good. Knowing Jerome de Guise and his beautiful, self-ish sister, I would submit that they are plotting mischief! Well, be on your guard, my dear. I shall scotch any rumors I hear, as indeed I have been doing. They are a pair, I know. I care not to have them for friends, but they would be much worse as enemies!"

She said little more, and they rested content-edly together until the Prince returned and ex-pressed his wish to leave. He kissed Rosalind's hand gallantly, thanked her for her hospitality, prosed for ten minutes on the beauteous women of Vienna and England, and finally departed.

It was already time for dinner, when more guests began to arrive. There was no time to talk with Adam, but his cheerful face and bright, flashing gray eyes told her there was probably good news. She was contented, as she swiftly changed to formal dress—a bright scarlet gown— and had her hair redone.

Adam was an animated host that evening, talk-ing in more lively fashion than usual, and Bar-naby Malloy contributed some stories in dry fashion of the days when he was in trade. Papa is becoming quite a favorite of Vienna society, his daughter thought proudly. They had come to ap-preciate his fine qualities, his blunt honesty, his wit, his practical common sense. More than one man had asked his advice about finance and the Exchange, and several ladies had professed to find him more amusing than the most flattering of Frenchmen.

The evening was late before the guests finally left. Rosalind was glad to retreat to her room and allow herself to be undressed by Norah. After the maid had departed, she sat down in a favorite golden chair before the fire, and mused on the evening. She was thinking about Clotilde's warning of the de Guises, when there was a tap on the door.

"Come in," she called, and Adam entered, dressed in night robe and gown, his face glowing and excited.

"I am sorry to disturb you, but I must talk. I have been boiling with the news all the evening, and was unable to tell you a single word, for it is in confidence!"

"Oh, but are you allowed to tell me—" she began, sitting up eagerly.

"The Prince said that I might—he trusts you, it seems!" And Adam smiled at her before throwing himself down on the couch near her. He sat informally, his legs crossed, his arm along the top of the velvet sofa. He began to tell her what had transpired, and she listened in some fascination.

It seemed that the Prince was now convinced that Czar Alexander would come around to the settlement of the Polish question in somewhat better manner than before. His position seemed to be softening.

"Germany is holding out for more; the Prussian state wishes to keep their part of Poland," said Adam. "But England will be on our side, we have some private assurances. And Talleyrand of France is striving for a balance of power. If Poland can be balanced against Saxony—" And he went on and on with the politics of it, bewildering Rosalind with the many intricacies. But he seemed to know what the matters were all about, and if he was satisfied, so was she.

Adam talked at some length. He seemed quite wound up, and needed to unwind before he could sleep. He changed posture a number of times, restlessly, sometimes sitting with his elbows on his knees, sometimes rubbing his aching thigh with a frown, as though unconscious of what he was doing.

"Ah, I have talked a long time," he said, looking up at the clock on the mantel. "Forgive me, you are such a good listener, I would talk on and on, as long as the Prince himself!"

"I don't mind at all. I am glad that you—trust me," she said, rather shyly. "Truly, I will not repeat anything of this. I am so glad that matters look better."

"And much of it is due to your friendship with Clotilde Denhof," said Adam. "We have been friends for a long time, and we respect each other. But she would not try so hard to assist, I believe, if she did not call you a close friend. I am very grateful that it is so."

He was standing now, and he held out his hand

to her. She reached out to meet his hand, thinking he was only clasping it in a good-night gesture. But gently he drew her up on her feet, and gazing at her intently, gravely, he drew her into his arms.

She gasped. She was enclosed in the circle of his arms before she knew it. She stared up at him, wide-eyed. Was he only grateful? Was he going to kiss her good night? She had gone stiff once more, awkward and alarmed at being so close to him.

"Rosalind—let us not be such strangers to each other," he urged quietly. "We have been married quite some time. I think our minds grow closer daily, I feel your gentle presence all about this house. When we go out in the evening, I feel the warmth of your interest in me and in my cause. Do you not feel this closeness also? I think you do."

"It is—not enough," she protested, her arms stiffening. He spoke no words of love, he did not pretend to love her. And affection and warmth were not enough; the shared interests were not enough for her starved heart. She wanted more, much more. She wanted love to match her own overflowing love.

"Not enough? I think you do not know of what you talk," he said, and drew her closer. His lips brushed against her flushed cheek, went slowly to her mouth, clung. She was held still for a long, breathless moment; then, with an incoherent sob, she pushed herself from him, trying to hold him at arm's length. But his arms were much stronger than hers, and he pulled her back again forcibly to him.

"Rosalind," he said, more sternly. "Do not be a child. I think you are a woman. Are you not?" And his lips pressed down on hers, more cruelly this time, harder, more roughly. She felt an unwilling tingle of excitement down her spine as he held her and one hand stroked down over her thighs, pulling her tightly to his long, lean body. She tried to turn her head. It only made his lips brush across hers again, and to her cheek. He bent his head lower, and his warm, hard lips went to her throat, down into the warmth of her shoulder, uncovered when the robe had slid aside in his roughness.

He was too close; her defenses were threatening to fall completely. With a last, final, desperate effort, she shoved him away, and held him away with her arms stiff at the elbows.

"No—no—do not—I will not let you—do not touch me—like that—" She blazed the words at him, outraged, furious at her own weakness.

He gazed down at her, shook his dark head abruptly, and let her go. "Very well," he said curtly. "Good night, Rosalind. But grow up fast. I do not mean to wait forever!"

And he stalked into his own rooms and slammed the door after him. She jumped at this unusual display of temper from the usually controlled man, and stared at the door for quite a minute before she ran into her bedroom and shut the door after her.

Chapter 12

The atmosphere between Adam and Rosalind
seemed abruptly to be more tense. At least, to her
taut nerves, Adam appeared to be much more
aware of her, to look at her closely when she entered a room, to gaze at her as he carried on a
conversation with her.

She felt jumpy, taut, angry at times that he
should affect her like this. The old easy relationship was gone, the calmness and gentle regard
that came from having a common cause. She
could not be at ease except away from him.

She went out more often with Clotilde, and
when her friend was not available, Rosalind went
alone to a café in the afternoon, to sit and think
over a cup of coffee. But she found this not so
easy as before. In her new, brilliantly glamorous
dresses, her smart hats, she was more noticed
than before, and sometimes men accosted her.
She could brush them away with a cold dignity,
but it was still uncomfortable.

Why, why did life have to be difficult? Before,
she had been plain, unnoticed in public, able to
go her own way in peace. It was exciting to be
considered somewhat beautiful, she decided ruefully, but it was also edgy. She felt as though she
were on display.

Outwardly, their life continued as usual. They

went out to tea, to dinners, to dances. They received guests at luncheon, at tea, at dinner, at evenings of music and conversation. Adam would shut himself in his study with one or more of his Polish friends, and they would talk politics by the hour, interrupted only by the appearance of other guests.

Rosalind found herself waiting, as though for a crisis, for something to explode, to make the uneasy calm of their life into something volcanic.

Then one evening they attended a formal grand ball at the palace of Schonbrunn. The Austrian Emperor, host to the Congress of Vienna, had invited more than five hundred persons to the ball. The roads leading to the palace were crammed with carriages for hours.

Adam had anticipated the crush, and in his usual foresighted manner had planned for their arrival in the early hours. He had instructed his coachman to call for them early, "or we shall be standing on the steps to all hours of the morning," he said practically.

As it was, the drive took two hours, and was accomplished by slow driving, with stops and starts that tried the patience of the spirited horses and the riders within the carriage.

Barnaby Malloy had not been invited, but he took the blow in good spirit. It was enough that his daughter had received a gold invitation delivered in person by a footman in a powdered wig. Rosalind was going up in the world, he had informed her proudly, more than once. He would have called her "Countess," but she had taken him severely to task for trying to do that.

"I shall stay home and have a cose with the Countess Constantia, with some good wine," he said happily. For he and Adam's mother were now getting along famously.

"You won't tire her, Papa," Rosalind had reminded him anxiously. Adam had listened to them both in some amusement.

"Nonsense, Mother enjoys your father immensely," Adam interrupted now. "She says he has more sense in his little finger than the lot of the Congress of Vienna!"

Barnaby's chest swelled. "I wouldn't doubt it! No other fellows have made anything in trade like I have!" he boasted. "I would like to see them on the 'Change! Lost, they would be, and dithering about trying to decide for weeks, while the opportunity to make money passed them by like lightning! If I had the doing, the Congress would have settled all the first month, and practically, too!"

"I think your father would have enjoyed this ball much more than either of us," declared Adam, as the carriage started up again. "We shall be crushed, unable to dance, standing in line for the buffets, having wine spilled on us, and that would be a shame on that lovely dress of yours!"

Rosalind smoothed the soft velvet of her ruby dress, under the black velvet cloak. "Yes, but I shall be careful," she said absently. "I know Papa would have enjoyed this. I think he should have gotten out of the carriage and directed the traffic, in a much more sensible manner! Whatever is the matter now?" she added, as the carriage jerked to a halt.

Adam peered out, and then drew back ruefully. "Close your ears, my dear. Two carriages have come together, and two gentlemen are not acting like gentlemen to each other!"

She had to laugh at his tone, and he talked easily to her to cover the oaths drifting to them from the crowded drive.

When they finally emerged at Schonbrunn, they found the palace lighted like a fairyland of beauty. The huge, lovely building, with its outspread wings, held carriages by the hundreds, and persons in huge skirts and formal evening garb ascending the wide, gracious stairs by the lights of the torches held by dozens of formally dressed footmen.

Rosalind felt unreal as she lifted her velvet skirts and, assisted by Adam, mounted the long staircase. They walked past footmen, nodded at other guests, spoke to the few they knew, and came to a formal entrance hall. They were inspected, their invitations glanced at; then they were directed toward one of a dozen rooms.

Adam was quite right. It was a crush. Rosalind could scarcely move from the room where she had left her cloak to one of the several ballrooms. She found Adam, or rather he discovered her, and slipped his hand onto her arm.

"I had best have a care of you, or I shall lose

you this evening," he said, as though it mattered much to him. "Come, let us find a little refreshment. The drive has made me quite thirsty. Would you fancy some punch?"

"Yes, I should." And they made their way to one of the buffet tables. Adam was deft at sliding in toward a punch bowl, and emerged triumphantly with two large glasses of cool delight. She smiled her thanks, and began to look about her with great curiosity.

Never had she seen ladies so grandly dressed, in elaborate silks, satins, brocades, and velvets, with their hair powdered or in jeweled high array. Jewels flashed on bare throats and bare arms—emeralds, rubies, sapphires, diamonds, in necklaces, bracelets, rings, tiaras, even in a few small crowns.

She recognized some of the British party at once, Lord and Lady Castlereagh among them. Talleyrand was made conspicuous by the fawning crowd about him, and she considered how different this was from the first days of the Congress. Now his very real power and eminence were beginning to be realized. Some said the very decisions of the Congress might turn about this ex-churchman, this strange Frenchman. Francis I, Emperor of Austria, was frequently surrounded, so that one could scarcely see his jeweled chest. The German princes were outstanding for their girth, she thought, and their bosoms held an amazing array of medals.

She spotted Metternich, and exchanged bows with him at a distance. He was escorting a lovely blonde lady. Later she saw Czar Alexander of Russia, and he had three blonde ladies with him.

"He does like variety," Adam murmured wickedly in her ear. He had been staying close at her side, and she was glad of it. She felt quite lost in the bewildering crush.

Fritz Dabrowski found them, and seemed glad to remain nearby. He soon asked Rosalind for a dance.

Adam refused for her. "Later, dear Fritz. The first waltz is always mine," he said with a smile, and put his arm about Rosalind's waist. As he swung her out into the crowd, he said, somewhere near her neck, "And I should like to claim them all!"

She felt flushed and hot, but was not sure if it was the tightness of her husband's arm, as he swung her lightly through the steps, or the warmth of the room and closeness of all the dancing lords and ladies.

Later she had her dance with Fritz, and he chatted gaily to her about the persons who were attending, the latest gossip about Metternich, something about a princess they both knew. He returned her to Adam, and they danced once more. Other friends claimed her hand, and Adam also danced with other ladies.

Still later, she realized she had lost track of where Adam was. Fritz was nearby, though, and she did not feel too concerned. She could see some other Polish and English friends, and Percy Eardley saw to refilling her punch cup.

Adam returned to her and took her in to sup-

per. He seemed grave and preoccupied, and she
wondered to whom he had been talking. He volun-
teered nothing, and she was too shy to ask.

As he had predicted, the lines were long, and
the waiting tedious. But there were always ladies
to observe, and their glamorous gowns, and their
escorts, and who was with whom, and the latest
gossip of the Congress. The hours sped by.

She was dancing with Jerome de Guise later on
when she realized she had not seen Adam for a
time. She began looking about for him. He had
said they would leave early to avoid the worst of
the crush.

"Unkind lady," said Jerome reproachfully.
"Can you not listen to my compliments? They
are meant most sincerely. Your eyes are as sparkling as brown stars."

"I never saw brown stars," she said practically,
in a tone designed to cool any ardor.

"I have," he sighed. "Oh, why did I meet you
too late? You were betrothed and married before
the rest of us could have a chance to meet you!"

"That is not true," she said promptly. "I met
you quite two weeks before I met Adam. But we
had little in common, you and I. You were always
talking of Paris, and I had never been there. And
you—" She stopped abruptly. She did not mean
to be drawn into intimate conversation with him.

"You mean I was so lacking in manners and
tact? Then it is all my fault! How could I have
been so blind to your charms? All I knew was
that you were a wealthy British heiress, that your
father was in trade. But, of course, I did not have

a title, and your father did not look in my direction."

His words stung, as he no doubt meant them to do. "Aye, the trade sticks in some throats," she commented drily.

"I did not mean for you to think I was after you for the money," he said with unusual bluntness. She glanced up at the hard black eyes, the considering look. "As some were," he added impertinently. "I was waiting to become better acquainted—"

To her relief, the dance ended. She made an excuse, and sought the company of some older Polish friends, talking to them easily until Jerome gave up and moved off after another bird of paradise, as he called them. She gave a little shiver of distaste as she thought of his murmured words, the way he had held her too close, in too familiar a manner. She liked him all the less, the more she knew him.

Czar Alexander paused near their group, and they all turned and curtsied to him. He was then accosted by a lesser nobleman, and they turned back to their own conversation. The Czar was for once without a lady on his arm. Rosalind, glancing at him, wondered if that accounted for the frown on his usually smiling handsome face. He was still quite young, and dashing.

Then she caught her husband's name. It was unmistakable.

The Czar was saying something about "Count Adam Potocki." Then he said it in a rapid question, ending with Adam's name. The nobleman nodded vigorously. The Czar turned, and went toward the nearest broad red-carpeted stairway.

Impulsively, Rosalind excused herself and rapidly followed him. She kept some twenty steps behind him, hesitating on the landing and looking back, as though not sure where she was going. The nobleman and the Czar went on into the next floor landing, and along the broad hallway.

She followed. She scarcely knew why, except that they had spoken of Adam, and something drew her on, some protecting instinct, some strong impulse of danger.

They paused at the door of one of the state bedrooms. As she came up to them, she saw the Czar had just entered the room.

Rosalind, at the doorway, was in time to see Adam standing with his back to the entrance, with Isabelle's arms about his neck. Isabelle de Guise, her black curly hair mussed, was pressing herself to his chest, her arms about his neck, drawing his head down to hers.

Both started as Czar Alexander spoke. "I beg your pardon," he said, in heavily accented English. "I have interrupted you!"

Adam turned about, so quickly that Isabelle was thrown off balance, and clutched at him to save herself from falling. Rosalind, watching, thought the French girl was not at all amazed, but rather triumphant.

Rosalind scarcely knew her own voice. It was high-pitched, shrill, but clearly enunciated. "Is this the room you suggested, Mademoiselle de Guise? I beg your pardon, I became lost in the maze of rooms. What was the problem you wished to discuss with my husband and myself?"

The others in the room turned to her. She was aware of the growing cynical knowledge in the eyes of Czar Alexander, of his bow to her. She saw Adam's face but dimly; he was impassive, strange, stern. Isabelle looked angry, baffled for a moment, before her gay mask slipped on once more.

"Your Royal Majesty," said Rosalind to the Czar, as though suddenly aware of his presence. She returned his low bow with a deep curtsy. "I beg your pardon. I was not aware of your presence for a moment. Am I interrupting your conversation?"

"Not at all, Countess Potocki. I myself seem to have intruded on a private speech between your husband, this lady, and—yourself." He smiled, and she knew that he knew what was going on. He gave her a quick little wink and bowed himself out of the room, speaking to the nobleman with him in Russian as they went.

Rosalind turned to Isabelle, and as she met the black, clever eyes, she knew she had a furious enemy. The woman was enraged.

"This problem you wish to discuss with my husband and myself, Mademoiselle de Guise," said Rosalind, with cool deliberation. "I am sure we can speak of it much more clearly tomorrow. We shall be at home tomorrow afternoon whenever you wish to call."

"Thank you, Countess," said Isabelle de Guise, with equal formality. "I should not dream of troubling you—now. I shall consult my brother, and several friends—as to how to proceed. Just a little personal matter." With a frigid smile, she swept from the room, her black curly head high, her skirts brushing past Rosalind's with a hiss of taffeta.

"The hour is late, Adam," Rosalind continued in a clear voice, conscious of curious passersby in the hallway. "I believe you thought we should leave early to avoid the crush. I am quite weary—shall we proceed?"

He came forward without a word, and offered her his arm. He was quite pale now, and there were beads of sweat on his forehead. They went slowly down the grand staircase, made their curtsies and bows to hosts and hostesses and other guests, and collected their cloaks.

At the entranceway they had to wait for their carriage almost half an hour. Rosalind thought she would never forget that time, standing at the head of the broad staircase, watching the footmen with their golden torches standing as still as statues, holding the lights for the gaily dressed crowd roaming up and down the stairs. The carriages drawing up, the high-stepping, shining horses, the sweep of ball gowns and cloaks, the wind blowing the fire in the torches—and all the time the frantic beating of her heart.

Their carriage finally arrived, and Adam escorted her down to it and placed her inside carefully. They were finally on their way. Behind them a long procession of carriages was drawn up.

"Thank you," he said finally, when they were

quite alone. "She meant mischief. I did not know how much."

"She sent for the Czar, I heard the message given to him. Adam, they are powerful enemies to you and to me, those de Guises," she told him deliberately, coldly. "You must be more careful with them, much more careful. I think they are the enemies of whom Prince Metternich spoke. For some reason they hate us, and they will frustrate the Polish cause. Whether it is personal, or political, or both, they are devilish, and will work their evil."

He listened to her with great care as she spoke of other incidents that had happened.

"Jerome de Guise has tried to woo me, kiss me in corners, make it appear we might be lovers," she said finally.

He started visibly, even in the dim carriage. "What?" His tone seemed to explode. "He has dared—"

"I too have had to learn my lesson. I was suspicious of him from the first," she said, in her cool tone. "He was too amorous too soon, too bowled over by my beauty. I did not believe him, of course, but did not conceive he could cause such gossip. But you know how Vienna is these days, rampant with mischievous stories. We should both have a care for our reputations, not just for ourselves personally, but for Poland."

"I fear you are right. But tell me of Jerome de Guise—what has he said to you, what has he dared to do?" His tone was vibrant with suppressed fury.

"That does not matter," she said decidedly. She did not want to stir up his emotions on that line. "It is over, and I shall not permit him any liberties. I dislike him immensely, and distrust him more. I shall not be alone with him, ever."

"I shall see to that," said Adam. "That he should dare—"

She settled back in her corner of the carriage. "He will not dare again," she said, in a tone that would finish the matter.

Chapter 13

Norah was waiting up for Rosalind when she came up to her rooms. The maid was eager to hear what had happened, about all the grand people who had been there, why they had returned early. Rosalind explained briefly that the crush had been so great they had decided to make their departure. "But they were never so elaborately dressed—you should have seen all the jewels." And she described some, to the maid's delight.

After Norah undressed her and left, Rosalind sank down into the small gold chair near her bed, to think and ponder a little. Isabelle de Guise had plotted this deliberately. What had she meant to gain? Probably their discredit in the eyes of Czar Alexander.

She was thinking of it so closely that the opening and shutting of a door scarcely caught her attention. She started violently when Adam entered the bedroom without knocking.

"I wanted to talk further with you," he said, frowning. "Will you tell me now about Jerome de Guise? Why did you not tell me before about his advances to you?"

"Oh, not tonight, Adam!" she said nervously, drawing her golden negligee more closely about her. His gaze made her feel jumpy. "Let us speak tomorrow." And she resolved to make very light of the incidents, if she could not distract him from questioning her.

"Yes, you must be weary. We will talk tomorrow. But I wished to thank you for your most clever rescue of me, the way you seemed to sense the danger. You are a most intelligent woman."

"Thank you," she said, subdued. When a woman wanted to be loved and adored, it was not much consolation to be told she was most intelligent. But she was being ungrateful, and roused herself to say more. "I wish very much to help with the Polish cause, you know this."

"You have been of much more help than I ever imagined you could be," he said earnestly. He sat down casually on the side of her bed, his long legs stretching out. She caught her breath and looked away from him. Oh, he did make it hard for her! She wished he would leave her room. Now he seemed to come in as though he belonged here!

"I am glad of that. If there is ever anything further I can do," she said with great formality, tucking her slippered feet under the chair, as he seemed to be gazing at them, "I hope you will so inform me."

"I have wished for some time to talk to you of our own personal relations," he said deliberately, gazing at her seriously. "You have seemed to avoid me more and more, rather than to come closer, as I had hoped. I know we married with great suddenness, and you were not quite willing that the marriage should take place so soon. Yet we have become well acquainted, and you are more formal with me than ever. This is not what I had wished."

Now she did feel alarmed. "Oh—I—I—this is scarcely a topic—to begin discussing so late at night," she said warily. "I am weary, we have had a long day—"

"And tomorrow you will run about with Clotilde Denhof, or bury yourself with menus, or discuss matters with the cook or the butler, and I shall not see you again until teatime! Really Rosalind, I do not know whether to treat you as a child or as a woman!" he said with great exasperation. "I try to talk seriously to you, and you evade with promises of tomorrow! We cannot put off our relationship forever!"

His patience seemed to have evaporated completely. With increasing timidity, she eyed his frowning face. She swallowed nervously, arranged her skirts for the tenth time, and fidgeted in the gold chair.

"Why do we not wait until the Congress of Vienna is settled?" she suggested, with a sudden wave of inspiration. "You are tired and have much on your mind, and I am anxious that things should go smoothly." She gazed at him hopefully, waiting for him to take this bait.

"I think the Congress could creep on until next summer or another year!" growled Adam, rising. "No. It has occupied enough of my time and energy. It should not so invade my personal life as well." He had come over to her, and was standing alarmingly close, so close that she felt the warmth and energy emanating from him. He reached out and put his hand on her shoulder, intimately, stroking over her bare neck. She flinched, and tried to shake him off.

"No—Adam—please don't do that!" she said breathlessly, drawing back in the chair.

"Why not? You are my wife."

His hand moved deliberately around her throat, closing over it, as though he could choke her, or draw the heart from her. It was too intimate, too frightening. Then he began to bend toward her. She caught a glimpse of his face, dark, flushed, his gray eyes shining.

"No, no, please—" She tried to wrench away. She pushed at him vigorously, with both hands against his chest, as he bent to her. She slid away with the desperation of an eel in a net, trapped, sliding past him, to jump to her feet and try to evade him. His arm slid easily about her waist, caught her back to him, thigh to thigh. "No!"

"Why not?" he asked softly. His other hand had gone to her mussed curly hair, and he thrust it up, his fingers caught in the curls, holding her face under his. She saw the determination on his face, the glint in his eyes. Then his warm large mouth pressed hard, cruelly, on hers, holding her silent for a long moment.

As soon as her mouth was freed, she wailed, "No, Adam, I will not let you— Oh, let me go—"

"Why? Why should I let you go? You belong to me, I should have claimed you long ago! My mistake was in waiting—you will not grow up until I make you," he said thickly, his Polish accent very strong now. "I think you will love me, you already feel some love for me—"

She was indignant, ashamed that she should love where he did not. Yes, he must know it, he knew the world, he knew women. Her secret was not a secret from him!

She sought for words strong enough to stop him. She would not yield to him, she would hate herself for the weakness. "I know why you married me!" she blazed, pulling herself up with as much strength as she could summon, wrenching her arms in an effort to free herself. "You married me—for the money—for the cause!"

His arms tightened; his eyes blazed down at hers incredulously, furiously. She was almost afraid. "I—what?"

"You married me," she panted, "for the money. I heard you—talking to Papa—and you said—the money—"

"How dare you speak of that? It was not—it was— Oh, I will not discuss it with you!" He was furiously angry, enraged, his face grim. "You have no understanding of this! No—no, do not pull away! We shall settle this matter tonight! No more waiting until tomorrow!"

She did not know later how she found the courage. But she said the words. "You married me for the money. How can I respect you, feel anything for you—when I know—it was the money? As soon as the Congress is over—I mean to return to England—and obtain a divorce!"

He glared down at her, his body rigid, as though the words were so many whip lashes on his body. Then he began to shake his handsome dark head. "Oh—no, no, that will not be! You cannot do this!"

She was fighting him again, desperately, though her arms hurt with the wrenching. "Everybody—knows it—they taunt me with it!" she panted. "The money—and Papa wanting the title. Did you both think it was fair exchange? I do not care about any grand titles! I shall return to England—to my *home*—and live alone—if I wish! I shall get a divorce—and you shall not stop me—nor Papa!"

"You—child!" he said forcefully, and of a sudden he picked her right up in his arms, one arm under her knees, and carried her over to the bed. He dumped her down, so hard the mattress bounced under her weight.

She glared up at him like an angry cat; she had never been so furious. She began to say, "You cannot stop me—"

Then she saw he was divesting himself of his

robe. She tried to get up, rolling over, flinging herself to the side of the bed hastily. But he was too quick for her, catching her and pushing her back on the bed, then following her down. He had her pinned against the pillows, and his face was very close, his dark, furious face, the gray eyes flashing with fury.

She fought him, with arms and legs flying, until he held her with his long legs and his long arms, pressing her into the soft sheets and blankets and pillows. She could not wiggle away from him; he was too hard, too powerful, too enraged.

She fought to keep her face from him. She could not evade the hard kisses on her throat and soft shoulders where he had pulled her robe down. She was half smothered by his weight, directly under him, her slim body helpless. Her soft breasts were crushed under his powerful hard chest. One of his legs was between her legs, and when she tried to move, he took advantage of it to move close between her thighs.

Alarmed, frightened, she knew then she had tried him too far. He was going to take her; nothing would stop him. He had forgotten all his politeness, his courtesy, his formality. In her bed, she was only a woman, and he a man who desired her—for whatever reasons were in his mind.

She whimpered, unable to fight him any longer. Her brain was spinning; she was dizzy, crushed beneath him, scarcely able to breathe. She went limp. His big hand was moving up the golden nightdress; her robe was ripped half off her. She felt the big hand on her bare thigh, caressing remorselessly, teaching her to forget the innocence she had known.

She turned her head restlessly, and his head came close to her once more, and he pressed his mouth to her open lips. She felt the warmth and wetness of his open lips, so surely, so softly, parting hers still further.

Everything had happened in a whirlwind. Now abruptly time seemed to stop. She lay while he caressed her, stroked his hands over her, made her shiver with his kisses, lingered over her softness, whispered to her in Polish words she only could guess the meaning of. He mingled love words in Polish and English. She was melting in spite of her fury and alarm.

She could not speak, she could not answer. No words would come. She turned her head from side to side, until his hand stopped her, his big fingers curling about her throat, holding her under his kisses. His lips opened against hers once more, and his tongue explored gently between her lips. She had never felt such kisses, never guessed at such voluptuous feelings as he roused in her.

Her eyes were half shut. Sometimes she glanced at his face shyly, when he was inches from her, absorbed in his caresses, and wondered at the passionate flame of his face. His eyes were glistening with passion; his mouth was sensuous, curled as she had never seen it.

Finally, he moved over her in a decisive way, lifting her arms to put them about his neck and shoulders, and he pressed himself on her. She gasped, and gasped again, and shut her eyes tight.

The pain came sharply, and she cried out. He paused and soothed her, and then went on.

She had never dreamed that it was like this, pain and pleasure so closely intermingled. The light kisses of his lips on previous occasions, even the tentative caressing of his hands, were nothing like this. Not even a prelude, not even a suggestion of the delights of the sexual contact of their bodies.

She was limp when he finally let her go and rose from the bed. She thought he would leave, but instead he blew out the candles beside the bed and came back to her. He pulled the covers about them, discarded her robe and his, and lay down again, pulling her into his arms as though he now owned her. She could not resist; she had no strength left.

She was so weary—so satisfied—so surprised!

She drifted off to sleep, aware only that he was very close.

She wakened once in the night, to find him stirring restlessly beside her. His arms were tightening; he was moving to lie over her once more. Automatically, her hands went up and slipped about his shoulders.

He murmured something in Polish, then in English. He teased her—"You have learned rapidly, my darling"—and a warm chuckle tickled her throat, where he was nuzzling.

His body moved slowly over hers. Her sleep-warmed body, relaxed and newly taught the delights of love, let his have its way, and she received her next lesson in sensuous delights.

She fell asleep again sometime later, knowing he was holding her, feeling protected, bewildered, strange, at peace, all at once.

The room was light with sunshine when she wakened again. She opened her eyes, to find Adam sitting on the edge of the bed, watching her gravely. He seemed quite relaxed and at ease, his robe on. She put her hand instinctively to her bare breast, and he leaned over and tucked the blanket about her shoulders.

"Your eyes are very big and brown, like velvet pansies," he said, as though accustomed to making compliments to her like that. "I wish to say something to you before the demands of the day come between us once more."

She blinked at him. She was not quite awake. "Oh—what?" she asked, striving to get her wits about herself.

"When I married you," he said, deliberately, seriously, "I was already in love with you. I loved you from the first, when we met and talked of horses—you do remember? Your eyes were so alight with pleasure in them, I thought how you would look when you loved. And so you do." And his finger flicked lightly against her flushed cheek.

"But I heard you—talking to Papa," she said stubbornly.

The gray eyes darkened; he frowned. "I do not expect you to believe me," he said, quietly. "But we are married. That is the fact. You may go your own way, I shall not check you. We respect each other too much to try to dominate the other. But I shall never divorce you."

"Oh—but—back in England—" she stammered.

"We shall live where circumstances direct us. It might be on my old estates in Poland, should God be willing that I regain them. Or in England, at your home in the forest, where you love to walk."

How could she resist him when he looked at her so gently and seriously? She glanced away from the gray eyes. Her mouth firmed. He had taken her by surprise last night, but it ought not to happen again. She had too much pride—

"I shall never let you go," he said finally, and rose from the bed. "Do not count on divorcing me. I do not mean to allow this to happen. Nor will you. Your faith, your religious beliefs, are against this. That aside, we are married for life. You may as well accustom yourself to thinking of this!"

He nodded, and went to the door. She was staring after him, when he turned about. Was there a twinkle in his gray eyes? Yes, she thought, in surprise and some resentment, there definitely was.

"Thank you for the delightful night in your arms," he said, and went out, quietly closing the door after himself.

"Well!" she gasped, and began to sit up. Then she was aware that she was completely naked, her nightgown discarded and flung after the robe. When had that happened? Sometime in that "delightful night," she supposed! "Oh—I don't know—what to believe!" she muttered, and scrambled out of bed to rescue the gown and put it on.

For a man who had married her for her money, he had given a rather convincing demonstration of passion, at least!

Chapter 14

Rosalind scarcely knew how to act the next few days. She felt like a new person, shy, strange, more aware of herself and of Adam, bewildered by the change in the relationship between them. She avoided him when she could, riding out with Clotilde, hiding away in the kitchens and the workrooms of the villa, coming out demurely for tea and dinner, trying not to look at him.

For when she did look at him, often she found his eyes gazing at her thoughtfully, his face softened. Sometimes he would be looking at the dress she wore, the way her hair was dressed, or at her hands or her slippers, as though studying her with new interest and appraisal.

He had not come to her room the next night, and she said she was thankful. The second night she lay awake for two hours after retiring, and wondered if the first time would be the only time, if he had taken her in anger and then been sorry—or indifferent.

Perhaps she had not pleased him. She did not see how she could have—she had been so ignorant, so stupid about responding. And—she tried to whip up her anger—he had no *right* to treat her like that, so possessively, so without regard for her personal feelings or her wishes!

She found herself each morning in a turmoil over what to wear. She would choose one dress, discard it, pick another of a more pleasing color or shape, try it on, until, to Norah's despair and wonder, she would have tried a dozen before she finally settled on one.

"Did I ever think to see the day," the maid grumbled, "when you would be hard to please like this? Sweet Mary, but you cannot know your own mind today! Now, that scarlet is lovely, or the bright blue—or the yellow—why not keep the yellow?"

"Do you think the yellow is prettier than the scarlet?" Rosalind begged, turning one way and another, twisting her slim form anxiously to see herself in the mirrors.

"It is beautiful, it is just right with your brown hair!" Norah declared positively, and Rosalind finally allowed her to dress her hair and wind a yellow ribbon through the curls, and send her down to breakfast.

She was rewarded with a bright gleam of approval in Adam's gray eyes when he looked up from the table. Her father growled, "Late again? This isn't like you, Rosalind. And will you be riding out once more?"

"Yes, Clotilde is coming about eleven, Papa." She busied herself with the teapot at her elbow, to avoid Adam's steady gaze.

"And you two will be riding about in an open carriage this chilly day in the Prater, all on the chance of talking to smart people!" her father continued to growl. "You have changed beyond recognition, Rosalind. You used never to care what people thought of you. Not that I mind," he added hastily. "I just can't understand what you see in this society parade. But that is your affair, your affair entirely."

She smiled at him and patted his hand affectionately. "I know, Papa. But that is the way of the world in Vienna today. It might do some good, Clotilde says. And yesterday we met and spoke with one of the German princes, and he was quite admiring and chatted with us quite twenty minutes."

"I don't know that I approve of that!" said Adam, unexpectedly, in his deep voice. "Perhaps I should accompany you today!"

She glanced at him, wide-eyed, met his amused gaze, blushed, and looked down at her plate once more. He was teasing, he really didn't care, she thought.

But somehow the warmth of his tone and his words lingered in her mind, and made her absent in responding to Clotilde that morning. Her friend teased her a little as they rode slowly along the carriage-clogged roads of the Prater.

"Your mind is somewhere else, dearest? Is it with that handsome husband of yours? You have the look of a woman in love! I declare that you do, with your cheeks so flushed and pink. No wonder the men are staring at our carriage today!"

Rosalind flushed at the unexpected attack, and could not look at her friend. She took refuge in her deep bonnet and gazed across the grass and trees until she was in greater command of her voice.

"Why—I—I suppose I have things—on my mind," she finally stammered.

A gentle gloved hand patted hers. "Darling, forgive me! I tease you too much. But he is indeed handsome, is he not? And so fine and strong? Sometimes there seems a coolness between you. Is he too formal?"

"Oh—no—no—" said Rosalind, too hastily, and Clotilde giggled naughtily, "I mean—he is formal, yes, but he—is most pleasant—I mean, courteous—polite . . ." She stammered to a halt. That night, he had not been polite, courteous, formal. He had been demanding, insistent, gently forcing a response from her, holding her in ways that made her blush to think of now.

"Good," said Clotilde, obscurely. "I am pleased. Oh, how do you do?" She smiled and bowed to someone. "Yes, indeed. And you do look so lovely in yellow. Did he comment on it?"

"No, he—"

"No? He does not notice your clothes?"

"Well, I think he does notice, I mean, he *stares* at me, and looks—I mean, I think he likes . . ."

To her relief, a young Austrian cantered up to them on his fine gray, paused at their carriage, and bantered with Clotilde. The subject was changed, others came up to them and spoke, and later they returned home for luncheon.

To her disappointment, Adam was not there. He had gone out with Fritz Dabrowski to see someone. He would return for tea, her father informed her.

Clotilde had gone home, and Rosalind had nothing much to occupy her mind but more menus and the household tasks, which had not been demanding recently. She was sitting in her own little drawing room, absently studying some accounts, when a footman came to her.

"Yes?" she said, rousing from her dreams.

"A note, Ma'am. The boy said it was urgent, to be delivered to you at once."

She tore it open. In a hasty scrawl, on plain paper, it said, "Dearest, come at once! Prince Metternich wishes to meet you just outside the Wolnar café, our favorite place—don't inform a soul! He has some important news for you—do hurry! Clotilde."

It was unusual, but Rosalind thought Clotilde must have written from the café. She tossed down the note and rang for her maid.

Within a few minutes, she was riding in her carriage toward the secret rendezvous. She kept wondering nervously if she would be capable of handling the matter. She should have waited for Adam—no, Clotilde had not asked for Adam. She wondered why Metternich wished to speak alone to her. She knew so little of politics. In fact, the more they discussed its intricacies, the less she believed she understood.

It was twenty minutes to the café, time for her to fume and fret, and twist her gray gloves to shreds. She alighted, and directed her coachman to wait. Then she went over to the café, rather timidly. It was early afternoon; scarcely a soul was there.

She looked about. The note had said outside the Wolnar café. She saw several carriages, but none of the markings were familiar. She had just turned to go into the café when a voice stopped her.

The man whispered, "Countess Potocki? This way, if you please. His Highness is waiting in his carriage—"

She turned eagerly to follow the man, who was dressed in some formal uniform. She followed him to the unmarked carriage, with its heavy curtains drawn. How strange, she later remembered thinking that the Prince should have arranged to meet me in this fashion. It was not like him, really.

She reached the carriage. The footman stood back respectfully, and someone from inside opened the door of the carriage. She bent forward to peer into the darkened interior.

Just then, someone behind her gave her a violent push. She stumbled. Someone lifted her into the carriage, and the person inside grabbed hold of her shoulders to pull her in at the same moment.

She was startled, frightened, and cried out. A hand was clapped over her mouth; she was held brutally to the floor of the carriage as it lurched to a start. Soon the horses were pounding over the streets.

She struggled in vain; two men seemed to be

holding her. She was on her knees, held cruelly in a painful position, one hand still clamped remorselessly over her mouth.

A trick, she thought in agony, a trick—someone—but who would do this? And why? She wriggled, trying to find a more comfortable position. She could not, and they did not seem to care when she whimpered in pain.

Then the carriage finally pulled to a halt. The door was yanked open. She was given a shove; someone outside caught at her and pulled her out rudely. She half fell over the steps. She was lifted upright, to stand before the man who slowly approached from the large house.

"You!" she said hoarsely.

"Countess Potocki," replied Jerome de Guise, his black eyes hard. "How kind of you to pay me a visit!"

"You—tricked—me—" Her voice was husky with fear, with the tightness of her throat. She brushed her hand over her bruised mouth.

"I am excited that you cared enough to come to me, Countess!" he said, a grin on his hard features. He gestured carelessly. "Bring her inside!"

Two men caught at either arm, and rushed her rudely inside the front door of the huge rented villa. She was out of breath when they deposited her in the large drawing room at the front. She whirled around when she heard the rustle of skirts.

Isabelle de Guise entered the room, followed by her brother.

"Mademoiselle," Rosalind said angrily, proudly.

"This is madness. Tell your brother to release me at once!"

The woman looked her over, the hard black eyes more than ever like those of her brother. "Why? We planned this carefully. No, you shall be our . . . guest for a time."

"Guest! No, let me go. You will be punished for treating me like this!" Rosalind could scarcely think, could not guess why they were handling her in such a brutal manner.

"Sit down, Countess," said Jerome de Guise. When she hesitated, he gave her a sudden push, and she sat down hard in a large chair and stared up at him in amazement. "Your eyes are quite pretty, so big and frightened. Yes, yes, I am glad we decided on this manner! I shall be quite entertained."

Rosalind took hard command of herself. Her heart was beating like a frightened bird, but she must, must be calm, she told herself. She took a deep breath, clasped her hands, composed herself.

"Would you explain, please, why you are treating me like this?" she said quietly.

"Oh, always the proper British lady!" Jerome de Guise mocked her, and his sister laughed, staring at her with hate undisguised in her face. "Yes, I shall explain! I mean to keep you here, my dear Rosalind! I think you shall be quite fond of me—shall we say, by the end of a week?"

"A week?" she asked blankly.

"Yes, I mean to have you for myself! You have become quite a little beauty, you know, blossoming out. I believe the good and formal and cold Count Potocki does not appreciate you sufficiently. I mean to keep you here, seduce you—to the pleasure of my love—"

"You mean to rape me," she said boldly, her hands clasped tightly.

"If you choose such a cruel word, yes," he mocked. "Rape you—ruin you completely!" And his tone became quite angry and cruel. "Yes, ruin you, Countess! And keep you here long enough for all Vienna to know you are here. Gossip flies so quickly about our fair city!"

She tried to keep them from seeing the shudders that ran through her slender body. But she felt they were gazing at her so closely, enjoying their verbal torment of her, that they could not help sensing them.

She kept silent for a moment until she could control her tone. "And why would you be doing that?" she asked. "What purpose? Do you hate me so much? It seems strange. I do not know what I have done to you to make you hate me so."

"Oh, not you so much." And Jerome's big tanned hand reached out and caressed her cheek hatefully, intimately. "But through you, I can disgrace and ruin Adam Potocki, the good Count! And he cannot interfere with our plans any longer! We do not care for his plans for the future of Poland!"

"Oh, so that is it," she said gently. "It does explain many things, the way you have been acting.

You are probably being paid a large sum of money to keep Poland divided and weak. Who is paying you?"

The caressing hand abruptly slapped her, hard. She could not keep from flinching, it was so sudden, but she stared at him with proud anger when he was about to strike her again. He held his hand back with an effort, his face suddenly grim.

"Little bitch," he said, and laughed aloud. "Oh, I shall enjoy this week! To have you in my bed, taming you—I shall be much amused! You are more woman than I had thought!"

"Jerome!" said his sister warningly. "Remember . . ."

He calmed down, and his black eyes gleamed. "Do not worry, dearest Isabelle. I do not talk too much! No, little Rosalind, the story is that I am much enamoured of you, and you have reluctantly returned my interest—hence, our rendezvous. By the end of the story which will go all about Vienna, all shall be in sympathy with my rapture over your charms, and in contempt of poor blind Count Potocki."

She could not keep the words from being spoken; they came naturally to her lips. "Adam will kill you for this," she said, quite simply.

He seemed to flinch; a flicker of something—fear?—came to his eyes. Then he laughed again, harshly. "I think not. We have matched swords before, my dear little Rosalind! And I have always won! No. Adam Potocki, through you, shall be disgraced and ruined, and Poland's cause damaged. And he cannot do anything about it—I assure you!"

Chapter 15

Strangely, though Rosalind was afraid, she was not in a panic. The thought of Adam continued to comfort her. He would find her. He would rescue her somehow. She kept thinking of him, of his calm, his courage, his protective gentleness for her, and it gave her renewed strength.

Her one hope for rescue, she thought, was to delay and divert Jerome. She sat back in the chair.

"Am I to be starved as well, Monsieur de Guise?" she asked, as though in idle curiosity.

"Starved?" He stared at her, his flushed face bewildered.

"Yes. I ate little luncheon. I am longing for tea. Your note—or your sister's—implied a meeting at a café. I quite thirst for it. Or is this not in your plan?"

He kept staring at her, then laughed a little. "Why not? We have a week to become closely acquainted, my little bird! Isabelle, order tea for our English miss!"

She frowned, began to speak; he flicked his fingers at her, and she quickly went to the bellrope. When a footman appeared, she ordered the tea

curtly, angrily, in French. Then she came back to
sit on the sofa. Rosalind calmly stood up, slowly,
so as not to alarm them, though Jerome was still
standing near her. She removed her gray cloak
and laid it neatly over the back of a chair.

She sat down, lovely in the bright-yellow dress.
She took off her bonnet, smoothed back her curls,
and adjusted the ribbon as well as she could. She
knew that Jerome was observing her closely, his
eyes traveling with insolent rudeness over her
body, studying her shape. She ignored him, as
though he were some crude boor who would soon
be removed from her presence.

She folded her hands in her lap and began
chatting with Isabelle. Though the French miss
fidgeted, Rosalind began to prose steadily on the
subject of art, music, the recent balls, the clothing
of the guests at the grand Schonbrunn-palace event.

"Did you ever see such jewelry?" she said. "My,
I quite admired the tiara of the Russian grand
duchess. One seldom sees such diamonds, such
emeralds. I believe the ruby is said to be one of
the largest in the world."

Reluctantly Isabelle entered into the conversation. "Yes, I have heard it. And her gown—covered with seed pearls and small diamonds. It
caught the light. I was quite covetous, and begged
Jerome for one like it."

"Too expensive by half, dear sister," drawled
Jerome, and to Rosalind's relief he sat down at
last, and drew out a cigar. He lit up, and was puff-
ing contentedly while the ladies spoke of gowns,
fashions, jewels. Rosalind had found a subject dear

to Isabelle's heart, and the Frenchwoman could not resist it.

The tea was finally brought. Isabelle poured, for all the world as though Rosalind were really a guest in their home. Rosalind wanted to laugh hysterically as the girl inquired seriously about her wants in cream and sugar and cakes, and Jerome sprang up to bring her the teacup and plate devotedly.

But she kept control over herself with thoughts of Adam. Surely he would miss her. But how could he guess where she was? She could not fight off Jerome; he was quite lithe and strong, and his footmen were all huge men. No, her only hope was in delay.

She spoke of the Vienna Congress and its gossip, avoiding the Polish question. She found that Jerome had fought in some battles with Adam, and questioned him eagerly about them. He began speaking of some battle on the Peninsula, and even Isabelle was enthralled at his description of the battle lines, the spying, the betrayal of some Spanish forces.

Rosalind's tea grew cold; she drank it and asked for more. They talked on and on, gravely, politely, while she ate and drank much more than she wanted. Anything to put off the moment of reckoning with Jerome de Guise. As she thought of his huge hands touching her, his greedy eyes studying her naked body, she would shudder, and seize upon another topic of conversation.

She heard a clock chiming three; later on, four o'clock. Still she kept up the conversation. Jerome was frowning now, but still amiable on the surface, talking on and on when she encouraged him by her interest. But he lay back in his chair with the litheness of a sleeping panther, waiting to spring when he chose.

Isabelle stirred, grew restless, glanced at her small gold watch. Rosalind thought of another item.

"Oh, there is a piece of gossip that might amuse you," she said, clutching desperately. "I heard recently from London. It seems that the Prince Regent gave a party at Carlton House, and when he invited the Duchess of—"

She drawled it out—making them wait for the climax—holding their interest with descriptions interspersed of events she had witnessed when royalty was present.

It was almost five o'clock. She had been there close to three hours, and she was growing desperate. How long could she hold off Jerome de Guise? She thought of appealing to his sister, but the Frenchwoman hated her, and would but laugh and sneer.

The ringing of the doorbell startled them all. Rosalind set down the teacup in her suddenly shaking hand.

"Let it go!" said Isabelle suddenly, turning white. "It might be—"

Jerome started up, too late. The footman opened the door to the drawing room, and in walked Adam Potocki and Clotilde Denhof.

Rosalind thought, Oh, thank God! And then she

saw the white, hard lines about Adam's mouth, and the fact that on his uniform he wore his sword—his field sword, not the dress one.

Clotilde came behind him, wearing her gray cloak over an elaborate toilette of emerald green. She had evidently been to some fine luncheon, for she wore emeralds and diamonds in her hair. Her look went first to Rosalind, sitting in the armchair with her teacup by her side.

Adam looked also at her, steadily, then back to Jerome. No one spoke for a long moment.

Then Jerome said, with a touch of insolence, "I was not aware I had invited you to tea! Only your lovely wife."

"I have come for her," said Adam gravely, in his deep voice. "Why is she here?"

"For tea," said Jerome, with a flicker of a smile. "As you see! We have become . . . quite close friends, eh, Rosalind?"

"Adam, he struck me on the face," said Rosalind, not standing. She sat quietly, fighting again for control against the hysteria which threatened to rise in her. "He kidnapped me in the carriage, threatened to hold me here, rape me, make sure all Vienna knew about it."

"Why?" asked Adam of Jerome. His hand was clenched over the hilt of his sword on his left side. "Why?"

"She is a lovely baggage," said Jerome, insolently, backing up slowly toward the mantelpiece. Above the mantel were several fine long swords on display. "She amuses me. And you do not appreciate her enough, Count Potocki!"

Rosalind said, quietly again, "They are being paid to wreck the cause of Poland. He hoped to disgrace you through me, to strike at us both."

"Ah," said Adam, and drew out his sword. "Clotilde, if you will take my wife from the room—"

But there was no time. Jerome had leaped for a sword behind him, and had it in his hand. Isabelle shrieked, and flung herself over to stand panting behind a chair as the two men faced each other. Clotilde grabbed Rosalind by the hand and pulled her over to the couch, to take refuge behind it.

"No, no, I did not think they—" whispered Rosalind, so appalled she put her hand to her mouth. "They must not fight—Adam—his wound—"

"Hush" said Clotilde sternly, and squeezed her hand. "Do not distract him! Hush!"

The swords clashed in a fine hiss as both drew back from the encounter to measure the other. Jerome had a tight, humorless grin on his lips. "I have bested you always! It will be the same, only to the end this time!"

Adam did not bother to speak. There was a tiger-like tightness to his face, to his lithe body in a slight crouch. He seemed like a slim black flash to his wife as he lunged forward, the sword shining silver. They parried, thrusted, circled slowly in a tight wary circle, watching each other's faces rather than the swords, taking the measure.

Rosalind was squeezing Clotilde's hand so tightly her fingers pained her, though she was only vaguely aware of pain. Her mind was on Adam, her thoughts frantically whispering prayers for him.

The room was silent, but for the hiss and clash of the swords. Two footmen were in the doorway, staring, not offering to interfere. Isabelle was crouched behind the chair, her fists clenched, her face ugly and afraid as she glared at the two antagonists.

Jerome lunged forward. Adam slipped to one side, recovered, crouched again warily. Jerome thrust once more, and the cloth of Adam's uniform tore in a slash from elbow to shoulder. Rosalind sighed, once. Narrow-eyed, Adam watched, waited—then lunged forward like lightning, and the sword struck home.

Jerome seemed to stand there, the sword piercing him through, as though held upright by the very force of it. Then he began to slide backward, clutching, clutching at the air, his face grimacing.

Adam pulled out the sword, and it came out red and bloody, dripping wet. Isabelle shrieked, and dashed forward as Jerome fell to the carpet, his head first striking a sofa, then sliding to the floor. Isabelle knelt beside him, trying to lift him up. Adam was staring down at them soberly, his wet sword in his hand.

"Jerome—Jerome—" Isabelle was sobbing, stroking back the black hair, trying to hold him up. "Help me, someone—help me! He bleeds—" She began to curse in French, shrieking for help. One of the footmen came forward timidly and knelt down. He fumbled at the bloody shirt. Finally he shook his head.

He said in French, "The master is dead."

Isabelle screamed, and fell back in a faint. Deliberately Adam bent over and lifted a cushion and wiped his sword on it. Rosalind looked at his face and shuddered. It was cold, hard, and expressionless as he wiped the sword free of his enemy's blood. He thrust the sword back into the scabbard at his side, and turned from the two on the floor.

"Come," he said to Rosalind and Clotilde. Rosalind felt paralyzed, but Clotilde pulled her forward urgently, toward Adam. Adam took Rosalind's hand, and they went to the door.

The butler opened it, and bowed them out as politely as though they had indeed come to tea. Yet he could not but be aware of what had just happened. Rosalind felt about to faint, but Adam's strong arm was holding her up.

They went out to the carriage, not speaking. The coachman started up as soon as they were settled, and they clattered away, the horses' hooves loud on the cobblestones of the driveway leading from the villa.

They went first to Clotilde's home. She broke the silence then, as they pulled up. "I will notify Prince Metternich at once," she said, in a tired, heavy voice. She touched Rosalind's pale cheek tenderly. "Little one, take care of yourself. I will notify you when I know what occurs. You may depend on me, Adam."

He escorted her into the house, then returned. Rosalind sat huddled in the corner of the carriage, miserable. It was all her fault, for being taken in by such a trick, she thought. Adam was so silent, so aloof, staring straight ahead, his face grim and set and hard.

They said nothing all the way home. She could think of nothing. She felt half sick with the tension and strain, and from remembering the sight of that bloody sword being withdrawn from the body of the dying man. But what if the dying man had been Adam? She put her hand to her stomach, gagging. He could be dead—her Adam—dead.

In the house, Barnaby Malloy rushed out to greet them. He gazed in concern at Rosalind's white face, at Adam's sternness.

"What in the name of heaven has happened to ye?" he blurted out. Rosalind put her hand weakly on his arm, tried to speak, then shook her head.

Adam said, still without touching her, "Go up to your room, Rosalind. Rest. I will inform your father. You must rest. Shall I send for a doctor?"

She shook her head, went to the stairs, and with head bowed began to climb up. She looked back once. The two men were standing watching her, concern on her father's face, only an unreadable blankness on Adam's.

She continued on to her room. Norah fussed over her, wanting to know what had happened.

She told her briefly, baldly, then began to weep. Norah soothed her, put her to bed, hovered over her.

Rosalind did not see anyone else that night. She slept little, feeling sick at her stomach, queasy, frightened. She was relieved that Adam had not been hurt—but, oh, what would happen to him because of this killing? And the thought of what the de Guises had meant to do to her made her ill once more.

In the morning she felt little better. Norah urged her to remain in bed. All the servants knew what had happened, she reported. The news was all over Vienna. Jerome de Guise had been killed, and his sister was taking his body back to Paris.

Adam came in as Rosalind was arguing feebly with Norah. He gazed down at her as she lay in bed, and she wondered if he even saw her.

"You must rest today," he said, gently but remotely. "You have had a considerable strain."

She wanted to ask, What about you? He had killed a man, one who had been a friend some years ago. How did he feel, what must he feel about that, as well as about the damage to the cause so close to his heart?

"What—has happened," she managed to ask.

"I have had a message from Metternich. There is a scandal, naturally. Metternich warns that we must return to England at once. We can do no more for the cause here. He urges that we pack, and remove within a few days. The British Embassy has sent an informal message to the same effect. Our papers and forms will be hastened to enable us all to leave."

She sighed, and lay back on the pillows. It seemed that everything had turned to ashes. "I shall—get up soon—and begin packing—"

"No, rest today at least. You are most weary. Your father is beginning preparations. He will have a care of my mother as well. We can manage. You must rest, Rosalind."

He spoke with concern for her, yet he seemed so remote, so distant, so uncaring, that her heart wept. When she did not answer, he went on.

"I am going out to see several men, to give them instructions and all the information I have gathered. I will be gone much of today and tomorrow. Then I too can assist in the removal arrangements. You will be all right today, I believe."

"Yes—thank you," she said, with difficulty. He bowed formally, as though he were in some drawing room instead of her bedroom, and left.

Alone, the tears trickled down her cheeks. She had wrecked his hopes by her stupidity. He would never forgive her for this. There could be no marriage between them, no love, no hope.

Chapter 16

Rosalind rested all that day. When Adam came into her drawing room that night, she heard

Norah tell him she was sleeping. She did not call out that she had wakened, but lay still as a mouse and let him go away again.

The next day, she rose and breakfasted in her room. Norah brought her the cards and notes of those who had called to express their concern for her. She read them, wept a little because it was so wonderful to have friends who cared, then settled down to plans for the next few days.

She must put away her own feelings and emotions, pack them in cotton wool, because they might never be needed again. For now she must concentrate on removing the household to England, making all comfortable for Adam's mother—she could do that much for him.

Rosalind began by consulting her father, and found he was moving things briskly. The footmen and maids had brought down all the trunks and cases, and were busily packing the linens and china. Then she went to see the Countess Constantia, whom she found in a rather nervous and anxious state. The little gray-haired lady clutched at her hand, pressed it warmly, and studied her face.

"Oh, my dear, I would not have had you troubled like this for the world. Those dreadful de Guises—how awful they were!" she burst out. "Oh, dearest Rosalind, you look so worn and so white—will you be able to travel?"

Rosalind tried to smile and comfort her. "Now, dearest, it is you we are anxious about. Will you be able to travel?" she teased. "We have several

large carriages, and you shall be wrapped about
in blankets. And our home in London is quite
comfortable—you shall have your own suite as
here. But if you would rather, we shall remove at
once to the country—Adam says you are fond of
the country?"

"Oh, as though it mattered—as though the
place mattered!" said the little Countess impatiently. But the color did return to her cheeks,
soft as white roses. "Wherever you and Adam are,
I shall be happy and contented. But my dearest,
this ordeal—"

"You are to forget it," said Rosalind firmly. "I
am sure it would distress Adam to think you are
fretting about it. And he is so immensely capable!
I know it was dreadful that he should have felt
forced to kill Jerome de Guise—but the swords
. . ." she could not restrain a shudder. "It was—
necessary. The fight began—there was no other
ending."

"Of course!" said the Countess, as though surprised at Rosalind. "Adam could do nothing else!
That de Guise should have treated you so—he
must have been in a fury of anger at him!"

Rosalind was a little puzzled that the Countess
should think in this manner. Adam's pride might
have been hurt, but he felt no real love for her.
Yes, that was it, he must have felt disgraced,
dishonored.

"But that is not the question now, dearest," she
said gently. "Shall I consult your maid about
packing? May we leave your trunks until the last

day? I want you to remain comfortable while we are in Vienna, and Adam has not yet said which day we are leaving."

"You must do just as you wish, I shall be comfortable," said the Countess, drawing her down to kiss her cheek. "Do not fret over me, dear girl. As long as you two are happy, that is all I desire."

Rosalind went away then, to see that luncheon moved ahead in spite of the upheaval of the household. Happy? That would be impossible now, she thought bitterly. She wondered how soon Adam would want a divorce. He had said—that night in his arms—he had said he would never give her a divorce. But now—now the situation was quite changed. She had ruined his ability to help the Polish cause. He could not forgive her for that, he would never come to love her now; all was lost.

Adam did not return home for luncheon that day, nor for tea. She and Barnaby sat alone, miserably silent. Her father had been terribly upset by all the events, muttering darkly about not being able to trust Frenchmen and letting his daughter put her head into danger.

She finally put down her cold teacup and tried to smile. "When are you going to pack the books, Papa? Your study must be cleared also."

"I might direct that now," he said grumpily. "Not that I have had a minute to read since I came to Vienna. A peculiar city this, isn't it, Rosalind? I'll be happy to get back to London. You know, I was just thinking. When we get back, I'll

stop in at the 'Change, and see what is going on.
Something sane in a mad world, *that* is! I might
go back into trade again; should you mind? Have
to have something for my mind to do!"

"You must do whatever you wish, Papa," she
said quietly. "You are very good at trade, and
whatever gives you pleasure is what you should
do. You know I am always proud of you."

"Yes, you are a good daughter," he said, with
dark gloom. "You were never one to say you were
ashamed of a father in trade, though your friends
were not always so charitable! Still, they came to
our house, didn't they, and ate and drank there!
We never lacked for company."

"And we never shall," she said, decidedly. "Just
think how popular you have been in Vienna,
Papa, with all the grand ladies asking your advice, and hanging on your shoulder when you
wrote down the stocks! And the gentlemen, too.
They did not despise the fact that you are clever
at money!" And then she remembered the conversation between Adam and her father, and such a
bitter, lost feeling came over her that she could
have wept.

But her father had cheered up. "No, they did
talk to old Barnaby Malloy," he said brightly.
"Remember the time at the dance of that Princess—what was her name? And the fellow come
up to me, and started talking money, and asking
advice, and here I was telling him all about what
to do, and he was a duke, yet!"

"I remember, Papa," she said, automatically.

Barnaby Malloy went off to his study to supervise the packing of his books. Rosalind finally went back to her drawing room. She had her own packing to supervise, and Norah had had the trunks brought down that afternoon.

It gave her a pang when the dresses were lifted out, the old grays and blues and pinks, and the new ones that Clotilde had helped her choose. They made such a contrast, the smart bright colors and the drab ones. Norah and the maid lifted them, smoothed them, wrapped them in tissue, and set them down in one trunk after another, the scarlet tissues, the ruby velvets, the orange and yellow and emerald-green ones. Would she ever have the courage or the desire to wear them in London? Or would she retreat alone to the house in the forest, and walk alone on the paths, or ride her beloved horses alone?

She fingered the smart black riding habit, the plumed hat with the scarlet plume. "Yes, pack these also, Norah," she said, with a sigh.

"Now, Miss, I'll but leave out a few things for ye to wear the next few days. Or ye'll have naught to wear on your back!" said Norah severely, and she kept in the closet the smartest and prettiest of the new clothes.

Rosalind sighed, and finally sent the servants away. She curled up on the sofa in front of the fireplace and gazed at the bright orange fire until her eyes blurred. What would happen to her? She could see nothing but gray in her future. Her father would go back to his trade and the Exchange, and she—to the forest. But the few memories she would have to live on would be a bitter, thin diet.

The door opened quietly, and Adam came in. She started up, and gazed up at him blankly.

"There you are, dear," he said, rather wearily. "May I come and talk for a time?" And he came over to sit beside her on the couch.

"Of c-course," she said. "Pl-please—and tell me—what we are to do? Have you d-decided when we are to remove?"

"I thought we would make a start on Monday— our papers are to be delivered by this weekend," he said, and stretched out his legs. He put one hand to his thigh and rubbed it absently, as though it pained him. There seemed more lines on his face, and she longed to touch his cheek and soothe him, and say absurdly nonsensical things to relax and please him. But he did not want her. . . .

"The packing is going well," she said into the pause, as he warmed his hands at the blaze and gazed absently into the fire, even as she had done. "I spoke to your mother, and she is quite reconciled to removing to London. I thought a suite could be arranged for her easily. I shall write at once to direct the cleaning and opening of the rooms—"

"Yes, yes, fine, Barnaby said as much," said Adam. "But I hope we two shall not linger in London. I quite long for the country, and you did promise me some good horseflesh to ride, did you not?" And he was actually smiling at her!

"Of c-course, Adam," she said, and tried to repress the aburd hopes that began to rise in her.

"But you—you will want—I mean—do you intend—I m-mean—" She stammered to a halt, unable to express her thoughts.

"Yes, we shall have to spend much time in London. I can work from there," he said.

She stared at him. He sounded tired, but not despondent—rather, alert and gathering his strength.

"Work?" she asked blankly.

"Yes. I have had a good long talk with Prince Metternich, also with Talleyrand, and our own ambassador, rather, yours—somehow I am identifying myself with the British," he said with an odd smile. "Lord Castlereagh was most encouraging, and gave me the names of several persons to contact in London."

"Oh!" she gasped. "Then—then all is not lost? I mean, you will be able to continue—"

"Yes, from London. I cannot remain here; Prince Metternich made that clear. But there is now hope of a compromise. The Prince is so angry at the way you were treated by the de Guises that he has generously offered to do all he can for our cause. He is quite fond of you, Rosalind, and most infuriated at the brutal and callous way Jerome de Guise meant to ruin your reputation, and treat you personally. He said it was dastardly."

"Oh!" she said again. "Oh—he is—he is—" And then she began to cry from sheer relief. She burst into sobs, burying her face in her hands.

To her further amazement, strong arms went about her, and she was drawn back against a hard chest. Adam's voice murmured soothingly in her ears; a soft handkerchief was pressed into her wet fingers.

"There, there, darling, you have had much to endure! I cannot but blame myself bitterly for not having sufficient care of you. I have let you run about by yourself—that I shall not do again!" he said firmly. "You seemed so independent, and so capable, I did not dream you would be deceived by such an old trick. From now on I shall have much care of you, and you shall do exactly as I order and arrange. Is that understood?"

She laughed in her tears, and cried in her laughter, but he seemed to comprehend her mood, and only hugged her the harder. Presently, he lifted her head against his shoulder so he could see her flushed, tear-wet face, and kissed it gently.

"I keep forgetting you are but a child," he said.

She was vastly indignant at that. "I am not a child!" she cried out passionately. "I am not! I am not!"

"Well, you may prove it to me, darling," he said mischievously, and his lips covered hers firmly. After a long, slow kiss, he finally raised his head. "You are growing up, yes, I do admit that!"

"Oh!" she said, rather dazed, and blinked at him. He bent and kissed the tears from her wet lashes. "But you—you do not want me! You will divorce me!" she blurted out. "You never loved me, and now—now you do not need—"

He frowned, and his mouth hardened from the soft sensuous line it had when he had kissed her.

"You will continue to talk nonsense!" he said, rather angrily. "I told you I will never divorce you! I realize you were reluctant to marry me, but nevertheless you did marry me! I will not let you go! You shall learn to love me in time; I will see to that!"

She blinked again, in a daze. He seemed to have everything backwards and upside down. "But—Adam—b-but—Adam—you did marry me—for the money—and now you do not need—I mean, the cause—and you do not love me—"

He scowled heavily. "I do love you. I love you madly," he said quietly, almost reluctantly. "I was—too proud to tell you of my love at first, because—I—well, I did need the money and assistance from your father for the cause. But I would not have offered for you, no matter how wealthy you were, had I not loved you."

"Oh!" she murmured in disbelief. "But, Adam —there were so many other ladies you could have married—"

"Exactly," he said calmly, his eyes twinkling. "I could have married others—there were some heiresses who let me understand they adored me—and the title! Including Isabelle de Guise. . . ." His face shadowed again, and he frowned. "Yes, let us forget that. You, my Rosalind, cared nothing for the title—at least I thought so. You cared for me—or I thought you did—"

"Oh, yes, yes. I loved you from the first," she blurted, then buried her crimson face in his shoulder. "That was why—I wanted to marry you—you did seem to care—and I loved—"

Firm fingers were set under her chin, and forced her face upward. Dark gray eyes studied her keenly, in wonder.

"You did love me? I was not deceived? Rosalind—tell me—you do love me?"

"Yes—I do—love you," she murmured.

"When did you first love me?" he demanded, for lovers must know.

"From the first time—when we met—and talked of the horses—and you looked down into my eyes," she said, not ashamed of that any longer. "I loved you then—but I could not believe you loved me—I am so plain, so—so ordinary...."

"Oh—you are my love," he said, and laughed a little. "You—plain? You do not see yourself! With your beautiful brown eyes like pansies, with your soft skin so inviting to my lips, your face, your mouth—your sensitivity, your gentleness—oh, Rosalind!" And his mouth came down on hers, with a hard, demanding, possessive questing that sent the burning heat of desire through her also.

When he finally lifted his head, she was out of breath, gloriously disturbed, breathing hard. He pressed her gently against the back of the couch, and rubbed his cheek against her soft cheek, and his one hand went lower, to hold her waist, to stroke over her thigh.

He whispered, "We have not had our honeymoon. Do you think we might leave my mother and your father to entertain each other in London while we retreat to that country home—alone? And ride about—alone? I long to kiss you under the trees, and lie with you on the grass—as I have wanted to do—before—to kiss you as often as I please—to have you to myself morning, noon, night...."

His kisses trailed over her throat, her shoulders, up to her cheek, then finally to her mouth, so she was unable to answer him in words. His lips were crushing hers, and she could only answer her lover by opening her lips, and responding—responding—as she had wanted to do for so long.